MW01484413

M TERESA CLAYTON

STORYTELLER

ART ILLUSTRATIONS
BY
R L HODGE

ISBN – 13: 978-0-557-77473-9

Edit Advisor: Debbi Zaicko

Published by

Lulu.com | 3101 Hillsborough St. | Raleigh | NC | 27607-5436

Printed in the United State of America

This book is dedicated to my Mystic family.

And to Gregory B Banks for your constant inspiration.

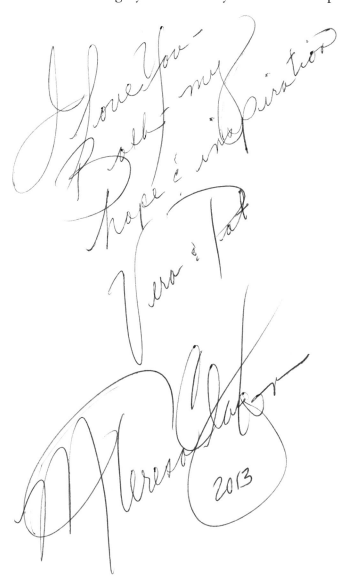

CONTENTS

FORWARD

From the beginning of time, we have been fascinated by fiction, myth and legend. As children we use our imagination to perform feats of magic, to be more than we are, to grow wings and fly. The answer precedes the question; what if?

Storytellers have been reaching beyond the ordinary for ages - channeling stories from somewhere beyond our own reasoning. After the story is told the questions begin. What if we could see what it is that whispers our name? What if there is intelligent life inside a drop of rain? What if we could navigate time and space?

These and other questions are asked within the stories told herein. A word of warning, the price of hearing the story is greater than the telling of it.

- The Storyteller

The Shore

Numb

…yet, I could feel the cool mist upon my cheek. I didn't remember where I came from. I had no idea where I was going to.

Nevertheless, there I was on a shore with the full moon's light glistening off the smooth surfaces of blue-white stones. I wiggled my toes against their satin-like finish. The cool surface felt good against the soles of my feet.

I took a deep breath.

The air felt charged with energy just like after a mid-summer storm. Yes, I thought to myself, I'm still alive.

Alive. What did that mean to me?

The clean salty air filled my lungs again. Inhale. Exhale.

As a hint of movement in the air brushed past my cheek I felt the warmth of my blood rush to the surface to greet it.

How did I get here? I wondered. *Here.* Where is here?

There was no sunshine, yet there was soft illumination as far as the eye could see. I looked up and felt the eerie feeling of being enclosed inside… of something. There were no clouds slowly ambling across this blue sky. No birds hanging aloft on the breeze.

No other sound, but for the waves gently caressing the opalescent shore. In and out, Whoosh… Whoosh…

Rhythmic… Hypnotic…

"It's a dream." I assured myself, "Just a dream."

Whoosh…Whoosh…I slowly turned my head to the left. All I could see was the endless iridescence of the white stone beach stretching out to meet the darkening sky.

I looked to my right. The shoreline was glowing in a surreal brilliance. Onward it continued to the horizon. I saw nothing moving in the light. I was alone.

In my left hand I held something. It felt like a medal, an amulet, a charm?

My right hand was limp at my side. I stretched out my fingers finding the cloth that dressed me here in this dream. I looked down to see. I was adorned in a white cloak that billowed with the slightest movement.

"A dream," I repeated to myself.

I looked down at my hand, it was as pale as alabaster; the perfect unblemished hand of a porcelain doll. Were these… *my* hands?

I placed my fingers to my lips. They were soft and moist. I could feel my breath on them as the air swept gently through them.

What am I? I asked of myself. Am I human, still?

The intensity of the light blinded me for a moment. It was coming from the sea. I could make out a tower in the distance. Appearing before me was an island across the great expanse. A lighthouse was its only occupant. There were no trees, no mountains; just the tower-light spinning slowly at its crown. Searching…

"…for me," I whispered.

"For you," he replied from beside me, "Only for you."

He was beautiful. He eased his way closer to me, careful not to frighten me. It seemed an odd meeting, the two of us on the shore, alone.

Where did he come from? I marveled.

I looked into his eyes. They were dark and his lashes long. They looked unreal, like a dolls eyes. Then he blinked and held me captive for another moment. I could not look away. His eyes seemed to hold lifetimes within them and I felt as if mine was becoming one of them.

He seemed to be searching for something in my eyes; perhaps something once lost.

Warm. His hand was warm. He took my hand into his own. As his fingers lightly folded around mine I felt a small shock tingle up my arm. I withdrew quickly from his touch, never taking my eyes from his; held fast in the spell.

Not a doll. He is human, like me, my thoughts confirmed.

"I have been waiting for you here for an eternity." He spoke quietly, his face tilting the slightest to reassure me, never looking away.

"Who are you?" I asked. "Where are we?"

"I cannot say." He whispered, leaning closer. "You aren't supposed to be here, it's not time."

He lifted his hand up to my face. I expected another subtle shock when his fingers touched my cheek. To my surprise it was a flutter I felt, not in my cheek, but in my chest. I closed my eyes and memorized the feeling.

I gasped once; twice… it felt as if suddenly there was no air. He closed his eyes and softly blew into my face and at once I relaxed once more into my breathing.

I could still feel his breath upon me. He balanced my chin upon his finger and pulled me to him. His lips grazed my own and I could feel the blood fill my veins.

Alive

My lips parted slightly to taste him. Sweet… His breath was sweet and I breathed him in.

His lips barely brushed against my own. I was losing myself on this faraway coast, not knowing who he was or where we were... but, I was surrendering, nonetheless.

"I cannot." He whispered against my breath and for the first time he looked away. "Not yet. It's not time."

"What are you talking about?" I asked, beginning to feel the panic rising in my throat. "I want to stay with you."

What did that mean to me? *Stay.*

"I have to leave you now, you must go back." He answered me firmly.

Then he turned to face me once more, "I will wait for you. I will keep watch from the tower for you." He reassured.

Was that a tear I saw tracing down his face and dropping silently to the ground?

"NO!" I cried out. "I want to stay with you."

"Forever... I'll wait forever." The voice faded into the mist.

Whoosh... Whoosh... the waves rolled gently in and then out again. He was gone.

I could see the hands on the clock hanging on the wall **3:00**. Was it morning or afternoon?

The smell of antiseptics filled my nose and sent me gasping once again for air. Whoosh... Whoosh... I can't breathe... something in my throat!

"It's okay, dear. You're okay." there came a voice from inside the light. "We're taking the tube out; you can breathe on your own now.

"Where did he go?" I coughed lightly. "Where am I?"

I could see her now. She was dressed in white; an angel?

The room filled with bodies, all rushing to my side. The room was alive.

I was alive. What did that mean to me?

Alive.

I was holding something in my left hand.

Remembering…

He waits for me on an island across the great expanse. He searches the shore with his tower-light…only for me.

Forever…

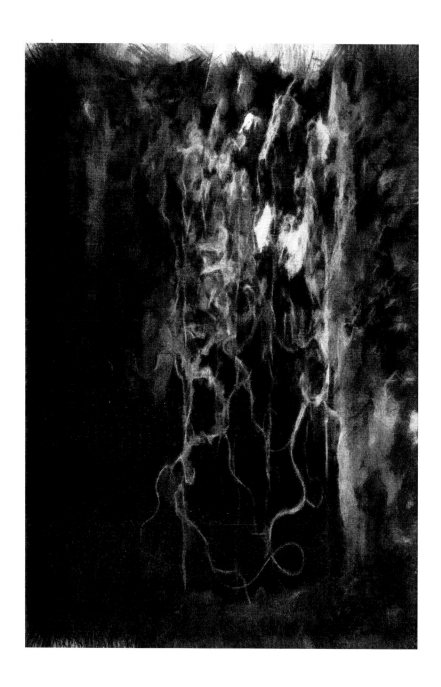

ALVA LEE

Alva Lee was only twelve years old when she discovered the cave, tucked away behind purple flowered vines, just a stones throw across Myer's Creek.

The sinewy flow of the creek had cut a lazy meandering pattern in the landscape, in and out of tall rock cliffs, down the gentle hillside, into honed out mini-canyons, through Mr. Carter's field and on down to Birch Lake. But, no one in Foster County had ever discovered this tiny doorway on the north cliff, which was now about a foot above the waterline, and shaded in vines.

Alva Lee did.

She was a small-boned twelve year old with eight little freckles that crossed over her nose and reddish-blonde pigtails that hung down to her waist in loose braids. She lived on a farm with her Ma and Pa, and little brother Doozy.

Doozy was a typical little boy. He was eight years old, almost as tall as his sister, and when he grinned all you could see was a mismatched bunch of teeth in various stages of development.

He was a bit of a worry for the family, "an accident waiting to happen," his Ma would say. Every time Doozy would have a mishap, and it happened several times a day, he would just shake his head and walk away saying, "that was a Doozy!" The family started calling all their mishaps *doozies* after their young son – and soon, he was stuck with the nickname for good.

The nearest neighbor to Alva Lee and her family was over three miles in either direction if you were to cross the fields on foot. When the water in the creek was a little higher Doozy and Alva Lee could float a ways down to the Carter farm. But, then they would have to walk all the way back home. So, straying far from home was not something they did often.

The days were hot, long, and dead quiet out there in no-man's-land. The rains hadn't fallen like they should, the creek was low, and the crops were dying from dehydration under the scorching heat of the July sun. Several farms were now looking for assistance from the "cash-strapped feds," as Mr. Carter would say. Everyone was worried about their crop. Water was getting scarcer and even a mud hole was impossible to find.

The chickens were getting sick and dying. Ma would put those that didn't make it onto small piles of dead grass and burn them just in case it was something that was contagious to the other livestock, or worse. But, she had to burn low so that it could be controlled with dirt instead of water.

The afternoons were the hottest part of the day and Alva Lee and Doozy would sit on the front porch trying to keep cool with a pitcher of Ma's home-made lemonade. The only sound you could hear was the excited whispers of Alva Lee to her little brother.

"I swear I saw a hole in the side of that cliff just past that old dead oak" she said. "It's hidden behind some vines, Doozy! We can reach it, I know it!"

Doozy's eyes grew bigger and he turned to his sister. "Pa says there's bats in caves, Alva Lee," Doozy whispered back firmly.

"We'll take the lantern from the barn and when we get to the opening we'll throw some rocks into it to see if anything moves," she reassured him.

"Do you think there are bats in that cave?" he asked her.

"I don't know, the cave has been underwater this whole time," she said to him.

"Snakes! There will be snakes!" he cried out.

"Okay," she put her hand on his shoulder, "We'll take a big stick and if we see one, we'll clobber it."

Doozy considered it for a moment weighing adventure against another day of hot incessant boredom. He just shook his head and, trusting his big sister, agreed to explore the cave the next day.

———◆———

After morning chores Ma called the kids in for their breakfast. Alva Lee and Doozy shoveled their eggs and ham into their mouths as if they hadn't eaten in days. "What's the rush?" Ma asked, looking from one to the other. "Have you both forgotten your manners?"

"No ma'am," Doozy muttered with full cheeks. Alva Lee slowed her chewing and put her fork down. There was no need to give Ma a reason to put an end to their plans.

After breakfast they helped tidy up the kitchen before asking to be excused. "Stay out of trouble kids." their mother called to them as they headed out the door.

Doozy and Alva Lee made a quick stop at the barn to grab a coil of rope and the lantern. "Matches!" Doozy reminded his sister.

She reached into her pocket, "Got 'em."

Now all they had to do was get to the oak without being spotted.

Under the dead oak that stood alone in the middle of the field they found two branches that had been blown down that were just the right size for them to handle and still be able to clobber a snake without getting too close. Doozy took the coil of rope from Alva Lee so she could hold her stick and the lantern as he continued along side his older sister toward the creek.

After walking a short distance he could finally see the curtain of vines covered in brightly colored purple flowers.

"Wow!" said Doozy, "When did this happen? How long has this been here?" The questions erupted quickly.

"I was walking along the edge of the creek bed and noticed the flowers. Aren't they beautiful?" she asked.

"What kind of vine is that?"

"I don't know, never seen that kind of vine before. Do you think it's one of those itchy plants?" She was referring to the poison oak that sometimes made them miserable for weeks. Their Ma would paint them with a mixture of honey and oats to soothe their prickly rash creating a whole new kind of suffering. "I don't know - you touch it first Doozy. See if it stings your fingers any," she prompted.

"I ain't touchin' it!" he said firmly.

"Okay, we'll both touch it together. Is that fair?" she responded.

"Yeah, I suppose it is."

The two of them carefully made their way down the sloping embankment and crossed through the knee deep creek water. Each was using their big sticks for balance. After they reached the other side, Doozy could see the mouth of the cave peeking through the veil of vines.

"It's a cave! A real cave!" her brother squealed.

"I told you, Doozy," she said. "Isn't it awesome?" she stated more than questioned.

"Here's what we'll do," she explained. "We'll each take a side and use our sticks to part the vines. When we get them pulled aside we'll hook them on the roots and other plants growing out of the side of this cliff here. Try not to touch it too much just in case it is an itchy plant. Okay, on three! … 1… 2… 3!"

Both of them lifted their sticks to spread the vines open just like Ma's living room curtains. They carefully latched the vines onto some of the roots poking out of the rock cliff, careful not to touch them.

Alva Lee and Doozy were now peering into a hole about six feet wide and four foot tall. They both looked at each other, sizing each other up, quietly wondering who would go in first.

"You're littler," said Alva Lee. "You should go in and see how far back it goes and see if we can both fit together inside the cave."

"You ain't that much bigger than me!" Doozy protested. "It's your cave… you discovered it… you go in first!"

"What if I get stuck?" she argued back.

"Take the rope with you and unwind it as you go. I'll hold this end and if you get stuck, tug it and I'll pull you out." he reasoned.

She knew she wouldn't win this argument so she dropped her shoulders and looked back at the mouth of the cave. "Okay, I'm going in. I'm no chicken heart." she said, hoping this would spur up some kind of confidence before she ventured on.

⬥

The ledge to the opening of the cave was about a foot over their heads. She would be able to climb up into it easy enough. They were both use to climbing things by now and Alva Lee was the fastest tree climber in Foster County.

Alva Lee took the rope from her brother and handed him the lantern to hold. She put her foot on a jutting rock and pushed herself upward. With the rope looped around one shoulder and her stick in hand she gracefully scaled the cliff side and perched on the ledge in front of the cave.

"Okay Doozy," she called down to her little brother. "Lift the lantern up to me and I'll reach down and grab hold of it." Doozy stretched his arm high over his head careful not to tip the lantern too much or lose his grip entirely. Alva Lee caught hold of the handle and with the lantern safely in her grip she sat up. "Here I go," she whispered under her breath.

She lit the lantern with one of the matches she brought with her, adjusted the flame and closed the latch. Alva Lee turned and held the lamp up in front of her. The cave looked so much bigger from this viewpoint. She picked up a stone and threw it into the cave hoping there were no bats. She listened but didn't hear anything, not even the sound of the rock falling onto the floor of the cave. With little hesitation she decided it was safe.

"Okay, Doozy – keep your attention on the rope in case I have some trouble." She said as she looked back down at him. "I'm going in!"

She took her stick and swung it from side to side in front of her. First high, then low – from left to right and then left again. She tapped at the floor in front of her. Nothing moved.

Alva Lee held up the lantern to light the area in front of her. There were no crags or roots in here, just the smooth skin of the cave. She continued, stepping carefully into the cave.

Once she was inside she stood up tall. The inside of the cave was much bigger than she expected. It was like a room, really, even the floor of the cave appeared to be smooth.

"Come on in Doozy," she yelled. There was no echo calling back to her inside the cave. "This is awesome, come see."

She could hear her little brother pulling himself up into the mouth of the cave.

"Look at this!" she said.

"This is unbelievable. Do you think someone made this place?" he wondered out loud.

"It looks like someone shined the walls, I can almost see myself in them," Alva Lee whispered, as if someone were listening. "It's just a huge empty room."

"Except for that!" squealed Doozy. "Over here!" He was leaping towards something that sparkled like a glittering bowling ball at the back wall. "What do think this is? It looks like diamonds! Do you think we'll be rich?"

Alva Lee approached the stone-like mass carefully, holding the lamp high and examining it closer with every step.

"Here is this huge polished room and the only thing in it is this big sparkling rock?" she mused to herself.

"Tell me it's diamonds and we are going to be rich!" giggled Doozy in his euphoria.

"I don't know what it is, really," she replied. "It sparkles so much I can't tell if it's a rock."

They were held in a trance by the glittering beauty of it. Doozy put his hands down on the dazzling stone and took a deep breath. "It's beautiful."

"Let's look around. Maybe, there are more of them. Let's start over here." She ordered.

She took the lantern and held it out in front of her as she circled the walls of the cave. The room seemed to be no more than ten feet high, ten feet long – and the room was shaped like an octagon. Lot's of little octagons.

She took note of the dry coolness of the cave wall, it felt like Jell-O and it appeared to be the same smooth texture on the ceiling. It was like…, Alva Lee thought, like a dull mirror – a huge octagon shaped mirror bubble!

Now that her eyes had adjusted to the darkness in the cave she could make out her reflection bouncing off one wall onto the other, up onto the ceiling, beaming her wide-eyed look of amazement right back to her. It was like being in a house of mirrors; unsettling.

The only thing that was close to normal was the cave floor. However, it wasn't muddy at all, which she couldn't understand. If, the water has been falling, wouldn't it leave the inside of the cave sludgy? No, this floor was solidly packed. She reached down to touch it with her hand; it was barely damp.

"Doozy," she whispered over to him urgently. "There's something wrong with this place. Caves are supposed to be muddy and wet with things hanging off the ceiling and coming up out of the floor. There's supposed to be crevices and stones lying about. There should be bugs crawling around, or a snake to slither through our legs; maybe even a bat or two. This place… this cave, doesn't even smell like a… cave!"

"Yeah, it doesn't smell like anything!" Doozy whispered back. "Isn't it supposed to smell wet or musty? I heard Ma say that caves had a musty smell to 'em."

"Come on Doozy, its time to get out of here," she urged. "I don't like this cave anymore."

"Okay, but let's see if we can get this diamond stone out and take it with us." he said to her.

Alva Lee wasn't keen on staying any longer, it was creepy weird in there and she knew they had no business exploring this cave. No business at all.

Doozy was using his fingers to dig into the ground next to the stone-shaped mass, trying to make room for his fingers to latch on and lift it out. He dug harder and harder, but the ground was showing no wear. It was solid.

"Alvvvva Lllleee," he stuttered, "The ground is vibrating, can you feel that?"

"We gotta go now Doozy!" she shouted "Now!"

He jumped up and the two of them made haste for the opening of the cave. Doozy had made his way past his sister and was all but diving out of the cave when his foot was hooked on something and he went sailing out the mouth of the cave and down into the shallow water.

"Oh my God!" screamed Alva Lee. "Doozy!"

She couldn't hear him. She was running after him when she saw it! One of the vines had made its way across the floor and it looked like someone had intentionally set it in such a way that it would trip someone. Like Doozy. "Doozy!"

"I, I'm okay, I think. Nothing broken. Ouch!" he answered.

Alva Lee climbed carefully down into the creek and knelt beside her brother. "Are you okay? Hurt anywhere?" she asked him.

"No. I'm fine. I think I did a complete somersault and landed on my butt," he laughed. "It was a doozy!"

"You tripped on one of those vines!" she snarled.

Alva Lee looked up at the mouth of the cave as she was speaking and her mouth fell open. She stood frozen there and Doozy let his eyes follow to where hers were looking.

"Alva Lee... did you do that?" he asked quietly.

"No." She answered him. "No I didn't do that."

The vines they had pulled back and hooked on the pieces of root jutting out of the side of the cliff wall had closed. The vines actually looked as if someone had placed each and every one of them side by side in neat order; hanging like a flower-beaded curtain.

"OK. Whatever is going on here, I want nothing of it." she said as she took her brothers arm and led him out of the creek, up the embankment and back onto dry ground.

Alva Lee and Doozy noticed they were leaving a wet trail behind them as they walked back to the old oak tree in the field. Alva Lee turned to her brother, "We have to let our shoes and clothes dry before we get home or Ma will tan our hides."

The two sat down under the old oak where they could rest after their walk from the creek and talk about what had happened in the cave. "We'll just rest here a spell until we dry out," suggested Alva Lee. "You are soaking wet!"

"You don't look as wet as me, Alva Lee," Doozy noticed. "How come I'm still so wet?"

"Hey, you're right! Maybe, because you were in the water longer!" she teased.

"You were standing in the water right next to me and your socks and shoes are drying out." He said making the comparison.

"But I didn't go completely under! You actually swam in the creek… but still, your shoes are still full of water and mine aren't." Alva Lee was trying to make sense of this when she noticed that the spot where her brother was sitting was now forming a little pool of water. Could all this water be dripping off of him?

She looked around for something to help dry her brother off with. There was nothing but the dried up grasses and the dirt. She took a handful of dirt and dusted his arms and legs with it. The dirt instantly became mud and began to thin in the water, finally dripping off of his arms and legs onto the ground where he sat. The pool beneath him was getting bigger.

"Don't move. Sit here and don't move until I get back." she instructed.

"Where are you going?" asked Doozy.

"I'm going to sneak back into the house and get some towels from the closet." She told him.

"My other shoes are down by the cellar," He told her. "They're dirty but they're dry. Do you think you can get them for me? I don't think these shoes will ever dry out."

They both looked down at his flooded shoes. His feet were swimming in shoes that were overflowing water.

"I'll be back as soon as possible, Doozy. It'll be okay," she reassured him, and to herself.

Where was the water coming from? Was it coming out of Doozy… or the shoes? Were they hexed or something? Her head was filling with questions as she ran back toward the house.

She stopped and looked back over her shoulder to where the tree stood. There was Doozy sitting beneath it, curled up into a ball with his knees to his chest.

For a fleeting moment she considered telling Pa and asking him to help. What would I say? She asked herself. My little brother is out there and water is oozing off of him and I don't know why? She thought. No, I can't say that. The questions that follow will only lead to more questions, and I can't tell him about the cave. We'll both be grounded for life! I'll have to fix this myself.

She was standing outside the kitchen door and looked down at her feet. She did not want to make footprints on Ma's clean floor with muddy shoes. As she looked down she noticed that her shoes were dry. No dampness. Completely dry and covered in dust.

No one was in the kitchen. She looked out the window and saw her Ma and Pa standing next to a small mound of fire. More chickens…She cut off the thought and ran up the stairs to retrieve two towels.

She skipped back down the stairs and stopped fast at the doorway to the kitchen. She heard voices. Ma and Pa were in the kitchen now. They were talking about the drought.

There's no drought out there under the big oak in the middle of the field, she laughed to herself nervously. No drought under Doozy, no indeed!

———◆———

She eased by unnoticed into the living room and exited the front door. As she made her way toward the cellar she looked up to see Doozy standing under the oak in the field. The heat from the ground was giving the appearance of Doozy standing in huge pool of water. Is this a mirage? She thought.

"Why is he standing?" Alva Lee wondered out loud.

She bolted for the cellar door, spotted the shoes, scooped them up and made the sprint across the field to her brother in record time.

"What is going on?" she screeched as she approached Doozy. "Where is all this water coming from?"

"I dunno Alva Lee. It's getting deeper and I'm sinking into the ground!" he squealed back to her.

"Move! Doozy, move!" she screamed. "Move out of it!"

"I am moving!" he yelled back. The water is coming from me, I think." He was trying to lift his legs out of the forming mud pit. The more he fought to move, the lower he sank into it.

She dropped everything and her eyes searched for a low branch she thought she could reach. She jumped; missed. It was too high. With all her strength, she pulled herself up the trunk and onto the first thick branch. She looked down at her brother as he was sinking lower into the ground.

"Hang on Doozy!" she yelled to him.

Alva Lee reached a dead jutting secondary branch and snapped it off. Holding the branch in her hand she made her way back down to the ground keeping clear of the forming pool.

"Here Doozy, hang on and I'll pull you out!" she told him. Doozy extended his hand out and caught hold of it.

"Be careful Alva Lee," he said. "Don't fall in!"

"I'm going to back up now Doozy and try to pull you with me," she added. "Here we go… slowly… slowly…"

As soon as she could see his feet were free she noticed that she was dragging him through newly forming pools of water.

She backed up more. The pool continued.

"We need to get back into the water, Doozy," she told him. "I think it will be easier in the water."

They hurried back to the creek and jumped into the knee-deep water together. "What is going on?" he looked at his sister with terrified eyes.

"I don't know," she answered cautiously. "Do you feel different? Can you feel the water coming out? What did you do, Doozy? Did you do anything in the cave?" The questions were exploding out of her as she was becoming more hysterical.

"AVLA LEE!" he screamed into her face to get her attention. "Alva Lee, I didn't do anything. We *both* moved the vines, we *both* went into the cave, and we *both* saw the glitter rock, we *both*…"

"You touched it, didn't you?" She looked into his eyes. "I didn't touch the stone, Doozy." She continued. "Did you touch it? Tell me. What happened? We gotta fix this, Doozy. We gotta fix this now!"

They started recounting their steps again slower, starting with when they saw the cave.

"The creek was low enough to cross – knee deep – still is," recited Doozy.

"The vines… the vines were over the opening and we pulled them back and hooked them on those roots right there." She pointed to the sides of the cave opening where some roots were jutting out.

"You climbed to the mouth of the cave. You threw a rock in to see if there were any bats. Nothing moved." He added.

Alva Lee spoke, "I lit the lantern and walked in slowly. I noticed the walls of the cave were so smooth. You climbed up and then noticed the "diamond" stone at the back of the cave. I looked at the ceiling and noticed it was reflecting my image back onto the walls and the whole thing made me dizzy." She continued, shaking her head to clear her thoughts.

"WAIT!" Doozy looked to his sister with an expression of dreadful knowing. "I did touch the rock. Me. I was the only one who touched the rock. It felt like it was vibrating real fast. It made my hand feel a little numb. I didn't really think about it much. It was so sparkly…" his voice trailed off.

"Look, Doozy," she pointed out, "Your shirt and pants are starting to dry off."

They were standing in knee deep water and now Doozy's once soaked clothes were almost dry. They both looked at each other and then slowly turned their heads in the direction of the cave. The vines had grown longer and were now skimming over the top of the water.

"I'm not going back in there!" Doozy's voice trembled.

"Doozy, step out of the creek water and walk back up onto the dry ground. I want to see if you stay dry." Alva Lee was trying to be calm.

The two of them slowly stepped out of the water and back onto dry ground. Just as she expected, a puddle was forming at his feet. His clothes began to feel moist, like he had been sweating hard after a long day of chores.

Slowly the two of them came to realize that they had to get Doozy back in the water, and fast.

"What am I gonna do?" asked Doozy trying to hold back the tears. "Please tell me I'm asleep and I'll wake up soon and this is all a bad dream…"

"Shhhh," Alva Lee quieted her brother. "Shhhh. Don't move Doozy. Be very still."

Alva Lee pointed to their legs. The water level had risen by at least two inches! "What is happening?" she asked herself.

Doozy began to breathe in sobs. "I'm gonna drown in the field or in the creek. It doesn't matter. I'm going to drown."

"You will not drown!" She was holding her little brother by the shoulders and shaking him. "Do you hear me? I won't let you drown!" Alva Lee yelled. "Settle down. I need to think."

"I feel something on my leg." Doozy whispered. His eyes were full of panic. "It's moving. It feels like a snake Alva Lee."

"Stay still and it will swim away Doozy," she said to him calmly. "Just stand very still."

They both looked into each other's eyes for reassurance. "Alva Lee?" Just then she looked down into the water and couldn't believe her eyes. The vines were stretched out into the water and were now wrapping themselves around her little brother's leg. She began to tug at the vines and tried to pull Doozy free. They were closing around him, wrapping him in their tendrils. The two of them were fighting to unravel the vines from Doozy's legs.

The water was now almost up to their thighs and moving faster against them. Alva Lee yelled to her brother, "I have an idea, Doozy. I'll pull them out of the ground at their roots!" With that she let go of her brother and pulled herself along the vines and up onto the ledge of the cave. She began to pull at the vines with all her might. The vines were anchored in the stone. They would not budge.

She turned around and began to pull at the vines that were in the water. Maybe she could pull her brother out of the creek and back up onto the ledge with her.

Without any resistance she slowly pulled Doozy to the side of the cliff. The vines had him wrapped in a flowery cocoon. She hoisted him up to her and quickly began to pull the loosening vines from his quivering body.

"They are letting go." he looked up at her with relief.

"Yes, I think they are." she answered to him flatly. "They, they seem to know what they are doing."

After she peeled the last of the vines from around her brother's leg, Alva Lee and Doozy fell down onto the ledge and laid there trying to catch their breath and possibly, wake up. No one said anything for a long time.

———◆———

"They held tight in the water but let go of you up here." Alva Lee finally spoke.

"Yeah, they did." answered Doozy. "It's like they want me here."

"Why?" asked Alva Lee to no one in particular, "What do they want?"

Alva continued, "We need to go back into the cave and find out. We need to retrace our steps and find out what we did to ... to ... make this happen."

"I don't want to go back in there, Alva Lee." Doozy said under his breath. "I'm afraid. What if we get in there and it doesn't let us back out. What if we never see Ma and Pa ever again? What if…"

He couldn't bring himself to say the words – we die in there?

"We have no choice Doozy," his sister told him. "We have to go in. The vines won't let us leave and you can't go anywhere dripping tons of water on the ground. You will surely drown then." There was a long pause between them as Doozy came to the understanding that his sister was right.

"Will you hold my hand?" he asked her weakly.

"Sure, Doozy, I'll hold your hand. I won't leave you. I'm right here and I'll be here with you no matter what." She assured him.

"I'm a chicken heart, Alva Lee, a chicken heart." He lowered his head and stared at the ground.

"This isn't about being a chicken heart, Doozy." she picked up his chin and looked into his eyes. "I've never ever seen anything like this. I don't know what's going on. But, I am not going to let anything happen to you, Doozy. You are a brave boy and what's happening here does not make any sense."

She continued, "Do you remember when you were about four years old and I was scared of the approaching storm? You took my hand and led me outside so we could watch the storm come in together. The lightning lit up the sky and the thunder boomed so loud. You held my hand and told me that this was God's fireworks. He was celebrating a new spring planting and was about to water the fields with his tears of happiness. Made sense to me… I haven't been afraid of storms since then, Doozy. You made it okay."

"Thanks Alva Lee, I'll try to be brave." he answered with a tear in his eye.

"Okay, here is the plan," Alva Lee said to him. "We don't have the lantern anymore so we're gonna have to feel our way to the rock. There aren't any bugs or bats or snakes, so we don't have to worry about that. Stay right next to me, Doozy, we're gonna crawl in and stay low. Got that?" she asked.

"Roger, over and out." Doozy saluted playfully. "What do we do when we get to the rock?" he inquired.

"I don't know, Doozy, we'll figure it out when we get there." She answered. "Let's go."

◆

They both got on their hands and knees and began to crawl slowly toward the back of the cave, being careful to keep some part of their body touching each other. Half-way inside, Alva Lee's hand touched the stick that she was using when they entered the first time. She must have dropped it in all the fuss when Doozy spilled out of the cave.

"My stick!" she exclaimed. "I found my stick!"

She picked it up and kept a tight hold on it as she continued to crawl forward. That's when she heard it; a low humming coming from the back of the cave. She didn't say anything to Doozy. They kept creeping forward. The humming was getting louder. Surely Doozy could hear it. Why wasn't he saying anything?

"Doozy?" she whispered. "Doozy, can you hear that?"

There was no reply.

"Doozy?" She could feel him next to her. She slowly got into a sitting position and pulled her brother closer. He was breathing. She could hear the humming with each breath, coming from his chest. "Doozy?" she asked again.

Still no reply.

She turned her head toward the back of the cave and began to see a small flicker of light coming from where the rock stood. It was coming to life. Doozy started crawling toward it as his sister began pulling at him to stop.

"Doozy, STOP!" she yelled. He kept pulling away, finally breaking free. "Doozy! Can you hear me? STOP!"

All of the sudden she could feel something wet running past her fingers and up over her hand. She withdrew her hand and smelled it. There was no odor. She apprehensively touched her fingers to her mouth. No taste. Water; had to be water. Was this coming from Doozy? Was he beginning to make water again?

She quickly crawled forward looking for her brother. She couldn't feel him. She took her stick and swung it slowly and gently from side to side hoping to find him.

The stone was getting brighter. A light lavender color was emanating from the stone. She could see her brother reaching out to touch it. "NO!" she shouted.

A wave of water spilled over her and caught her unguarded. She spit and choked on the water as it found its way into her throat. The wave took her body and in one swoop lifted her and pushed her out of the cave and into the water of the creek below. She went under. Fighting to right herself, she finally broke the surface and shook the water out of her eyes. Alva Lee was shocked to find the creek much deeper than it was before…

Where was Doozy? She looked to the mouth of the cave and water was spilling out in a torrent. Surely Doozy was swept away with the first wave. She began to look around for her little brother.

Alva Lee swam for the cave's entrance. Gotta find Doozy, she said to herself. The vines. I'll pull myself up on the vines.

That's when she saw it. The vines were all reaching back into the cave. "What are you doing!?" She screamed. "Leave my brother alone!"

The water outside was now over the opening to the cave. She could feel the floor of the cave with her foot as she waded back in against the force of the water.

Alva Lee could hear the humming coming from the back of the cave… and below the water! "Oh my God, Doozy!" She kept yelling.

There appeared an eerie pulsating purplish light beneath the water. She could see her feet through the water as it was rushing by. But, the water was rushing in too. It was pushing and pulling her. She could see her little brother surrounded in vines. They had wrapped themselves around him again and were lifting him out of the water.

"Alva Lee?" he sputtered, "Alva Lee, is that you?"

"Doozy, can you hear me?" she asked in a panicked cry. "I don't think they want to hurt you. I think they are helping you. Hold on and we'll let the vines take us out of here."

She was right. The vines seemed to be carrying Doozy out of the cave and out into the creek. She caught hold of the vines and swam along side of them.

When they got to the opening she could see that they only had a few more feet and the cave was going to be under the water again.

The vines carried Doozy to the side of the creek and began to untangle themselves from around him. Alva Lee ran to his side and began pulling at the vines. They were humming. And, Doozy was humming back to them!

His eyes were wide open and unblinking. "Alva Lee, they don't want to hurt us. They just wanted me to return the chip."

"What chip?" she asked him.

He reached into his pocket and pulled out a small glittering light about the size of a pea.

"What is that?" she asked again.

"It chipped off of the big diamond rock in the cave. I wanted to keep it. I thought it was magical. It was singing to me and it made my hand feel warm." He answered her. "I don't know what it is, but they want it back."

"Then give it back to them, Doozy!" she ordered him.

One of the vines stretched over to where Doozy was holding the chip in his balled up hand. He slowly opened his fingers and the vine gently removed the stone from his open palm.

The water was getting deeper and they couldn't see the cave opening anymore. It had gone completely under the water. The vines were retreating back toward the cliff side.

Doozy was still humming along with the sound emanating from beneath the water. Alva Lee could see it now. There, far below the water's surface, was that strange lavender light. It was humming louder. She could hear the vines as they vibrated their own low humming. They were all participating in this crazy choir.

"What's going on?" she asked her brother. "Do you understand what they are saying?"

"Don't be afraid. They're saying, don't be afraid." He answered her between refrains. "They want to go home."

"Who are they?" she asked him.

As Doozy continued to make a guttural humming noise, a voice emanated from within the sound. "We are life-forms that exist inside the water, air and the light, Alva Lee." The voice was not entirely his and it was mixed with the humming somewhere inside of him. "Water contains the energy of many lifetimes. We nest in caves like this one when the water-ways begin to dry up."

"Life-forms?" Alva Lee couldn't believe her ears.

"Imagine millions of little prisms bouncing light off of a rainbow and each sparkle you see contains life. These water spheres huddle together and create this glowing twinkling mass. We wait for the rains to come so we can resume the journey. And, then you found the cave…" his voice trailed off.

"Who are *WE* and how does Doozy know all of this?" She wasn't sure who she was addressing but the only one standing in front of her was her little brother.

"They're telling me things, showing me things," he answered her in his own familiar voice.

"The vines? That humming. Are they talking to you too?" she asked hesitantly.

"The vines are created by spores that attach themselves to the water droplets. The vines protect them from invaders, like us. They are a shield, but we got past them and entered the cave anyway." He said in that strange humming voice.

"They tried to stop you from leaving!" Alva Lee thought aloud. "They tripped you, remember?"

"No." he replied gently. "No. They just wanted the chip I took returned. It's wasn't time for them to return to the source yet."

"What is *the source*?" she asked him.

"They say they are leaving now. They have to go." He explained to his sister. "They want us to go home. The rains are coming." He said to her and began his humming again.

Alva Lee grabbed her brother's hand and pulled him along with her out onto the field. They stopped to pick up the towels she dropped onto the ground earlier when she saved Doozy from sinking into the mud. She needed to collect her thoughts.

Alva Lee sat down beneath the old oak tree. "I don't understand this at all." She pondered out loud. "Why were you making water, Doozy? Now you aren't, but before…"

"The chip." he answered soberly. "They wanted to go back. They just wanted to flow back to the source. Now they are together again. I'm not a vessel any more."

"A vessel?" she asked. "Big words for a little boy, Doozy. Are they still talking to you? Are those their words?"

"Yep. Their words." He answered. "They are leaving soon. Do you have any more questions for them? Better ask now."

"The cave walls! The cave was almost a perfect octagon and the walls were like a smooth cool gel, and I could see myself! And, the floor of the cave, packed and solid…" the questions were exploding out of her mouth. "I don't understand any of this!" she shook her head in disbelief.

The humming picked up momentum. She could almost feel the weight of it coming from the air all around her.

"We are carried within the droplets of water. We move from vessel to vessel making our way back to the 'source' where we start anew. When the vessel begins to empty we must find a place for ourselves to rest. The caves serve as resting places for us to gather and wait." The voice was not coming from Doozy; it was inside the humming sound that was all around her. She could understand it. It was in the air and it was talking directly to her.

"Some of us take on another form, a mist, which expands all around us. We are surrounded by a protective seal that cannot be broken easily. It's like living on the inside of a jewel. There are many facets there. The facets inside reflect light and sustain the lives within us…" The voice continued.

Alva Lee couldn't believe it. The humming was coming from nowhere and yet, everywhere. The air was beginning to feel damp with the approaching storm. It was electric and alive!

"We travel with other life forms that we release into the air if the cave is exposed above the water's surface. They are our guardians. Once our barrier is crossed, light and air collide and mix with our matter, creating various levels of the color spectrum." The voice was fading.

"Spectrum? Facets? Vessels? I don't understand it all, but I think I know what you're getting at. You're alive and you just want to make it home… to the source, as you call it." She was finally communicating with nature. Doozy had his eyes closed and he was giggling.

"We travel the waterways until we are called home. We eventually return to the earth and start our journey again. Perhaps we serve to replenish the earth by feeding the plant-life, or by being consumed by the animals. We are essential to life on this planet; therefore, we must be on our way." As quickly as the humming started, it stopped. It was gone. They were gone.

"WOW! That was a DOOZY!" Doozy yelled out. "I don't know what they said, but I know what the meant!"

"No one is ever going to believe us, Doozy." Alva Lee said. She turned to look toward the house in the distance. She could see the faint outline of Ma and Pa in the kitchen window. Out over the horizon she could see the storm coming. "We better get home now."

Doozy was staring back toward the creek. It was getting higher. The storm northwest of them was filling the creeks and streams with new water; new life. The drought was over.

Alva Lee and Doozy snatched up their things and ran out across the field for home.

———◆———

"Goodnight Alva Lee. Goodnight Doozy." Their Ma and Pa called out before settling down for a long night of much anticipated rain.

"Goodnight." the kids called back to them.

"Water. Who would have ever thought that water was… alive?" whispered Doozy into the dark room.

"They just wanted to go home. They wanted to go back to the source." replied Alva Lee. "Do you think the source is the same thing as God?"

"Everyone wants to go to heaven. And, heaven is… up there." Doozy answered and pointed to the ceiling. "Makes sense to me."

The room was quiet for a time. Finally Alva Lee spoke, "Now I lay me down to sleep. I pray the Lord my soul to keep. I ask not for myself alone, but for all thy creatures – every one." To which Doozy replied, "Amen."

Postscript

1) Scientists say that every drop of water contains some remnant of the past within it. We could be drinking the same water that quenched the thirst of dinosaurs.

2) Microscopic life-forms abound in a single drop of H2O, constantly moving from continent to continent - from the northern polar ice-caps to the rain-forests of South America.

3) The Earth is always communicating in a low humming ambient sound. Astronauts can hear it and our satellites can pick it up both from the ground as well as out in space, and measure its tone.

4) And, who is to say what the source is? Our earth is protected in an atmospheric bubble of its own as we orbit our Sun. Galaxies spin through the Universe. Perhaps we too, will someday return to the source.

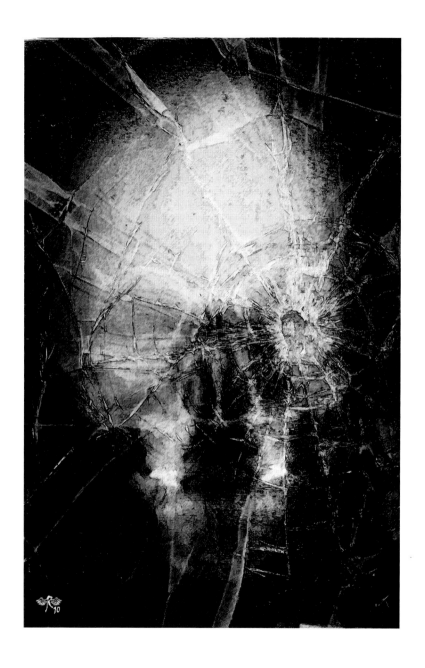

COLOR OF RAIN

I sit here looking out this broken window glass wondering about trivial things to pass the time; like, whatever happened to the public phone when it only cost me a dime, one little dime? What happened to *a penny for your thoughts*, do they cost more to produce now than then? It was simply a saying that suggested that someone else took an interest in them.

Where do whims take us? Imagination seems like such a nice place to go. A place of wonder and enchantment, how could anyone choose to say no?

Sweet dreams sound so sugary and pink, I prefer a grittier story-line; a darker mystery to hold my interest and a handsome hero would be so divine.

This crack in the window, how was it done? Perhaps a stone or misdirected baseball - except for this little hole in the middle here… won't appear to be accidental at all.

Rain; funny how it drops in so many colors, sometimes rainbows of tears drop from every cloud. But, my favorite color of rain is that lavender hue. It's a subtle color, not too bright or too loud.

When will people begin to notice the changes that have taken place all around? Perhaps we need to make changes of our own before we are put into the ground.

Whose idea was it to create destruction, arguing that it provides us with more than it takes? Doesn't that depend on the person who sits at the desk and the decision that he solely makes? Let's hope he has many good days filled with laughter; hate to send him to work angry or feeling a bit off. Worse, hope he doesn't hit the wrong button trying to cover that nagging cough.

There is a slight aching in my head where I was hit by the bullet shot through the pane. The glass cracked and all I remember is the endlessness of sky and the peaceful color of rain.

My ability to communicate is getting harder to do. It's my mind, it's foggy and there's some interference. Today's rain has a funny smell to it and the taste is bitter too. Lavender rain smells fresh and clean, there's quite a big difference.

I'm going to lay my head down against the window glass and enjoy the wondrous view of life from up here. I can see my past lives marching by on parade; nothing ever gave me reason to fear. I'm sure I'll die right here on my window seat, looking back on those yesterdays surely missed. This has taken me quite by surprise; I didn't imagine my time would end like this.

Goodbye to neighbors and companions who gave their time and love generously. Whoever shot the bullet, he doesn't know it found a target and never intended to shoot so carelessly.

So take him and wash him and give him absolution, tell him about my life and what it meant to family and friends. Tell him one bad choice - not a bad man make, but to own it and remember how this moment ends.

Ask yourself, son, what is the color of rain? Look out into the storm and see what is there; rain drops of every color falling to the earth painting dreams of hope everywhere.

Dance in the rain; don't you mind the storms. Paint colors of rain upon your skin and dance; rainbows of life renewed, if we give each other a chance.

THE CLEARING

She was seventeen and up till now she took the voices for granted; whispers, really. Perhaps they were a figment of her imagination. Perhaps she was over-hearing a conversation carried upon the breeze.

And those movements in the shadows, just beyond her peripheral vision, disappearing from view when she would turn to catch them. She was certain they were there. Still, she dismissed them.

She and her best friend Kelly had often entertained the notion of another realm just beyond their senses. It was common knowledge that dogs could hear the high-pitched sounds that human ears could not. Elephants could hear sound much lower than the human ear could detect. A hawk can see a mouse from a mile above the surface. And some people believe cats can see spirits.

She remembered once listening to her aunts and uncles talking with her mother about a time when her grandmother was gravely ill. Grandpa had passed away some two or three years before and yet, grandma spoke with him as if he were sitting right there, on the edge of her bed.

They said it was the medication. They said it was old age. And, some entertained the thought that maybe, just maybe, grandpa was indeed there.

Sara often took walks with her best friend Kelly. They would walk the woods at dusk and listen for the movement of the animals as they began to come out of their hiding places for food and water. The deer always seem to know when the girls were getting too close. They would dart away; white tails held high like flags signaling a retreat.

"I hear voices, sometimes," Sara said to Kelly on their walk back to the house. "Have you ever heard voices, like your name whispered, or someone saying STOP before you are about to do something that would hurt you?"

"I did when I was younger," Kelly answered, "but since I've gotten older, I don't think so. My mom says it's just our mind playing tricks on us."

They walked on up to the house and Sara said goodbye and waved as Kelly drove off for home.

The following morning Sara saw the movement in the shadows again – just out of view, from the corner of her eye.

"Is someone there?" she asked.

She closed her eyes and tried to think of something else. There was a whisper coming from over her left shoulder. What is that? She asked to herself.

She opened her eyes and without looking behind her, she walked toward her window. Again, she saw something move in the shadows of the room. Was it the tree outside her bedroom window, dancing with the sunlight, which gave the illusion of something or someone there in the shadows?

"This is ridiculous," she murmured. "The next time I see or hear something, I'm just going to ask it what it wants with me!"

Just then she heard the voice again. It was suddenly clearer. "Sara."

"I'm not afraid of you." She called out in a brave voice.

There was no reply.

She softened her tone and began again, "I just want to know who you are and what you want. I don't think you are a bad spirit or you would have hurt me already. Please show yourself."

"Sara." The whisper came from just behind her. She swung around; no-one was there.

"Sara." it whispered again.

This time Sara closed her eyes and whispered back, "I'm Sara. I can hear you. Please talk to me. I'm not afraid."

"Walk with us Sara." The voice seemed to blend into a chorus of voices yet it was barely more than a whisper. "We can show you things that will change your life. You can tell everyone that we are here with them and want them to know us," the voice was coming from nowhere and everywhere at once. "They have to believe, listen, and see beyond the limitations of their senses – beyond the limits of their reasoning.

Slowly she headed for the door. She didn't even stop to take her jacket. Her excitement was all she knew.

"Go to the clearing, Sara," instructed the faceless voice. "In the clearing we will show ourselves to you and tell you all the secrets of our world to help you in yours."

Sara slowed her pace just before getting to the clearing. What am I doing? she thought to herself.

"Don't give up on us now, Sara." The voice replied.

It could hear her thoughts!

She entered the edge of the clearing and saw movement toward the center that resembled a small dust devil glittering as it swirled in the sunlight.

"Close your eyes and I will lead you," whispered the voice. "Follow your senses; the ones that resonate deep inside of you."

She closed her eyes, took a deep breath, and began to walk slowly at first. Then she was jogging. It wasn't long before she was running in full stride, eyes closed and feeling free. She could see the clearing in her mind's eye, hear their voices, see their form and she was filled with an incredible joy.

One voice spoke, "That's it, Sara, believe." While another whispered, "Can you see us now?"

Sure enough, as she stopped in the center of the clearing and without ever opening her eyes, she saw them. Perfect creatures, almost human, dazzling bright and giggling with happiness at her arrival there. Each one came up to her and offered a gift.

"These are the gifts of light that man has rejected over the millennia since the world began," one said to her. "You are one of the few believers who have been unafraid and have come to meet us."

Another told her, "Man has limited himself by his senses and we can no longer communicate our gifts to him. Mankind is given these gifts of light at creation then slowly fade and are lost to mankind's doubt and logic."

While yet another added, "Please take these gifts and share them so that all of mankind will know them and gain understanding of all that is seen and unseen.

She could no longer feel herself standing. She was not sitting or laying down either. She was floating. It seemed her eyes were wide open and she was being carried inside a bright sparkling light. Sara was shown compassion, mercy, love, peace, enlightenment, truth, and many more of the things man had long forgotten. Yes, there were the *words*, but the *essence* of those words expressed was lost. Here she felt all of them, all the graces, all the gifts, all the secrets that would enable man to live peacefully enlightened upon the earth once again.

There would be no need for fighting, jealousy, envy, greed, wars… ever, ever again. She was so overcome with happiness that she cried tears of joy.

After the spirits had presented all their gifts to Sara, they asked her to please go out and share this knowledge with everyone in anyway she could.

She ran home.

Once inside she sat her mother and father down at the kitchen table and began telling them of her morning in the clearing, meeting all the spirits there and receiving the gifts and knowledge they entrusted to her.

Her father looked to her mother with a look of worry. The two of them had expressions of deep concern on their faces.

"What's wrong, Daddy?" she cried, "Don't you... believe me?"

"Mom?"

Both of her parents reassured her that it would be okay. Yet, it was understood that they did not believe her.

The next morning Sara's mother came to her and told her they had an appointment with the doctor. It seemed that her mother feared the worse; that Sara was losing her mind.

Doctor Flannigan came in and sat down across from her.

"Explain it to me again, Sara" he said in a low condescending voice. "I want to make sure I hear you correctly."

Sara told her story again and again... to this doctor and that doctor, until she was overcome with so much sadness and despair that she quit telling it altogether. Sara was beginning to doubt herself.

Did she really hear them and see them? Did they really give her, a small-town no-body, all the gifts and knowledge to save mankind? Quite possibly, she *was* crazy.

Sara was admitted to the hospital that day and found herself locked away in a small room with a bed and nightstand. Nothing but silence filled the air. And sometimes, the voices would come to soothe her and offer her hope.

I'm going to be in here for a long time, she thought to herself. They think I'm crazy and maybe I am.

"We won't be able to talk with you much longer," whispered the voice. "I'm so sorry they are doing this to you. Again, the limitations of man have compelled him to silence our voices."

The door clicked with the sound of a key in the lock and the door opened. The nurse came in and gave her two more pills. Slowly she was beginning to forget her voices and soon she would not be able to hear them at all. She was so depressed by this loss but soon that would be erased too.

Weeks went by while the doctors regulated her medications so she could be released to her parents and go home.

When Sara finally came home she numbly went up to her room and sat on the bed.

"All in my imagination," she whispered to herself.

"No! They were not a figment of your imagination!" the voice came from the hall. It was Grandmother! "Listen to me, Sara" she said as she came into the room and sat next to her on the bed. "I hear them too. And I can see them from time to time."

"You do?" replied Sara. "You know?"

"Oh, I've heard them and seen them many times. The older I get, and the more I lose of my sense of sight and sound, the more I see and hear them. They are everywhere."

"But Grandma, I can't hear them or see them anymore. The medicine has taken them from me. I failed. I didn't even have a chance to spread the good news and tell everyone what I learned." She sobbed into her hands. "I failed at offering their gift to save mankind. I don't even remember much of it anymore, it's gone."

"Oh, sweet girl" Grandma reassured her as she stroked her hair. "Someday you will hear them again and see them everywhere. If you were unable to share the gifts you mustn't blame yourself. Mankind, including Mom and Dad, choose to believe that there is nothing but what they have right under the noses.

There are no possibilities for them and the many, many others like them. They will all perish without any wonderment in their lives. You and I cannot make them see or make them believe."

As the years passed, Sara was finally taken off the medications and went on to have a family of her own. She would take her children often to the clearing in the forest. In the clearing they would close their eyes and let their imaginations soar. They would talk to the spirits there and fly in the air on glistening pillows of light. They would talk for hours to the faceless voices of light and Sara would let them fill her children with all kinds of wonderment.

Then on the way back to the house, Sara would tell them that imagination is a wonderful thing - you can go anywhere and do anything. All you had to do was close your eyes and open your mind.

———◆———

"Do I believe? Sara pretended to carefully consider the question posed to her. "Hmm. Why, YES! I do believe! I believe in all the things and in all the possibilities of what life can be when we aren't confined by mere science, man-made beliefs and so called facts of life. We always *KNOW* but we choose to *NOT BELIEVE*."

So for generations, her children's children and their children's children passed on the gifts given them in the clearing. However, time and conventional wisdom would silence the voices as they grew up and slowly erase the memories.

But for Sara and her grandmother; they would enter the world of the "other side" when their times came. They would dance and sing and be eternally happy among the spirits of the clearing. They would become part of that shimmering "light"; their voices becoming one as they whisper each of our names, calling us to close our eyes and believe.

STORYTELLER

"Black cats… unlucky, that's what they say about 'em. Don't let one cross your path." The old man was almost faced-down in his drink… "They say, if one steps in front of you, just turn around and walk th' other away. Whatever you do, don't look back!"

"Harry, what the hell is he talking about?" Someone shouted from the other end of the bar.

The dust covered bottles that lined up in front of the mirror had long forgotten how to reflect their sharp staggering images. The mirror itself was covered in a brownish yellow film from years of heavy smoke and the occasional thrown drink. There was a crack that splintered from the bottom, across the last third of the mirror and out the top. If you looked at it just right, tilting your head a little to your left and squinting your eyes slightly, it looked like an old woman hunched over, in silhouette.

The bar was long and ran the length of the room. Three tables, each one had a matchbook under one leg for balance, with mismatched chairs were lined up along the facing wall. There was barely enough room for a man to walk between the tables and bar stools. Maybe this was done on purpose. It stood to reason that you could get shit-faced drunk and still be able to stagger upright to the loo without once losing your footing.

Tess was a regular here. An attractive woman, she never seemed to sit on her stool, but rather perched there; her long legs pooling over the edge of the seat. She came in about ten every evening to mingle with the other well established members of this *lonely loser's* club. She always left alone.

Marv and Al were roommates living in the apartment above the tavern. They came in every night for exactly four beers each before politely excusing themselves and heading upstairs. It had been decided years ago that the two were much more than roomies, though it was never confirmed.

Burt was a large man. He held court every night at the far end of the bar. His seat was sagging from years of abuse from his ample backside. It was also the only bar-chair in the place, made of imitation black leather, with a swivel! He expounded on a multitude of trivia without much debate. It wasn't like Burt to ever sit quietly and listen to the jabber amongst the other barflies. He was a book of useless information.

There were several others who would stagger in on their way to another bar two blocks away. There seemed to be a tavern on every other corner in this part of the city and the drunks would work up a thirst meandering from place to place. Eventually they would have to find a comfortable spot to lie down and snooze it off. Park benches were definitely out of the question, as were sidewalks; loitering was breaking the law. However, on cold winter nights, it behooved a sotted soul to be carted off to the pokey for the guarantee of a warm shelf to lie on and a dried up cake donut with black coffee in the morning before they were shuffled back out onto the streets.

I was a newbie. Not new to drinking, just new to this part of town. This made my third visit to **Harry's Hangout** on the corner of Hample and McArdle Street. This tavern didn't look much different from any other on the north side of town, but those others didn't have Tess.

I was put out of the house by my, now pending, fourth ex-wife. Jobless and unmotivated, I managed to set up temporary housing at the shelter several blocks away. "Getting on my feet." I assured the man at the reception desk of what was once a cozy hotel lobby before becoming the *Saving Souls Mission*. Yeah, right.

My first wife ran away with my best friend, my second with my sanity, the third with *her* best friend and the fourth was making away with my soul. I didn't have anything else to save.

The only thing I made away with was two plaid shirts, one pair of jeans and one pair of underwear. I managed to get my shoes but totally forgot about socks. The young lady I was with that night barely got out alive.

"Black cats? What does this guy have against black cats?" the question on everyone's mind was finally thrown out there by someone at the bar.

The old man at the far table looked like death warmed over. He kept up his sermon on black cats all evening, stopping long enough to throw a glance Tess' way.

Who wouldn't want to look at her? She was stunning and definitely out of place here in **Harry's Hangout**. Still, she didn't really seem all that interested in me or anyone else here. Try as I might to make conversation she always gave me the standard two or three word answers. Definitely, not interested.

Harry hobbled his way down to Burt and replaced his empty bottle with a new cold one. Without so much as a word, Harry picked up two quarters from the bar top in front of Burt.

Turning to make his way back down the length of the bar to the cash-register he looked up at Marv and answered, "I have no idea, he's been babbling about cats for two weeks now!"

I asked Harry what the old man's name was.

"That's Charley." He grunted. "He must have got hold of somethin' bad about two weeks ago. He came in here one morning shakin', eye's lookin' a little crazy, and talkin' 'bout some kinda shape-shiftin' he saw the night before out back in the alley."

Something… *bad*? Did I hear him right?

"Drugs?" I asked.

"That or somethin' worse." Harry chuckled. "He was never nothin' but a drunk so far as I know, but the story he told me was outta-this-world! Must be drugs or the man's brain just shorted out!"

"Superstitions!" Tess spoke out from behind her Gin-Rickey with a slice of lime.

Charley froze and stared at Tess for a moment then looked down. Did I see a hint of fear on his face?

"Something about a black cat, a woman, drums, and then she just vanished into thin air! Bam! Gone!" Harry shook his head, "I dunno, it was some sort of hallucination if you ask me."

"Is the whiskey goin' bad?" Al suggested.

"That man's insides are pickled in cheap alcohol!" laughed Harry. "It ain't the whiskey… no, this ain't nothin' of the drinking variety."

I looked over my shoulder toward the man slumped down in his chair. Charley. He seemed like any other drunk I'd ever seen, maybe he was just misunderstood. Lord knows I was misunderstood. We had something in common, so I ordered two shots of the cheap stuff with beer chasers. I had a story to listen to…

"Heard you had an encounter with a black cat!" I spoke as I sat down across from him, "Name's Jack, glad to make your acquaintance." I extended my hand for a shake. He just looked up at me and squinted his eyes for a moment.

"Yes sir!" he said after a long pause to size me up, "Cat-woman. That she was!"

"A cat-woman you say? I'm all ears, Charley… and I'm not superstitious… tell me about your black cat-woman." I prodded him.

"I'll admit I was sotted, but no more than usual and I don't do no drugs!" he assured me in a stern voice, pausing long enough to shoot Harry a look before he continued. "I'm not crazy either!"

I wasn't so sure, but I'd sit through anything at this point to cut the boredom. And, it didn't look like I was getting anywhere with Tess.

Charley's story started with a whispered introduction, "It was closing time and I knew I'd have to find a spot out back and hunker down 'till mornin'. There are a few guys who make it a regular habit to get some shut-eye in the condemned remnants of the garage behind the bar, but it was such a nice night and the moon was full… I decided to catch some Z's in the alleyway that night so I pulled some bags outta the dumpster and made me a pillow to lay my head on…"

Charley took a deep breath and coughed. Was it my imagination or was he aging right in front of me? I decided it must be the light, or lack thereof, back here in the corner.

"It was about three o'clock in the morning," he continued, "and I was staring up at the most beautiful sky I'd seen in years. It was so… peaceful…" He stopped and threw back the shot of whiskey, then wiped at his mouth with the back of his hand. "The full moon was casting odd shadows in the alleyway. Hadn't really noticed it before, but then, who am I but an old drunkard barely capable of noticing whether or not I've pissed myself."

Charley stopped and tilted his head as if he were listening for something. I watched him closely for a moment and noticed a small twitch run across his face.

"Charley, you okay?" I asked him.

"I'm fine," he assured me and went on with the story, "I had this edgy feeling, like you get just before someone hits you over the head and runs away with your last dollar. You get a sixth sense about things when you take to the streets."

Charley looked up at me for some sort of validation before continuing. "Though the alley was glowing under the moon's light, there seemed to be something moving in the shadows. I couldn't get a focus on it. It kept moving from one side of the alley to the other, crouched low, and coming closer."

I could see that Charley's hand was shaking. He hesitated, seeming to catch his breath, "I don't remember passing out there, nor waking up! It was more like I was hypnotized or somethin'. Again, Charley looked up. He didn't see me this time; he was looking in Tess' direction. I let my eyes follow his. Tess was still facing the bar seemingly disinterested with Charley's story. Harry was busily emptying ash trays. Marv and Al were silent and still. Burt was mumbling to himself about some war.

"I listened for some sort of clue but couldn't hear nothin' out of the ordinary..." Charlie explained. "I gotta tell ya, son, I was shaking like an old man with palsy! I could sense it, there was something coming and it was getting closer." Again Charley stopped to listen. His hand was shaking noticeably now.

I called over my shoulder for Harry to bring us another shot of whiskey. The story was getting interesting and I wanted the storyteller to relax and remember every detail.

Charley coughed hard a few times. I thought he might have actually spit up into his lap. Then he spoke, "Out of the blue I heard this high shrill scream. It didn't stop either. I wanted to cover my ears but couldn't move my arms. That awful sound would fade a bit and then come on strong again. Sounded like one of them hyenas at the zoo...or a cat being gutted...a cat...black cat..." he coughed again and slammed back his shot of whiskey.

The old man closed his eyes and when he opened them again I could see the popped blood vessels turning the whites of his eyes to red. He stared into space without batting an eye. I thought I'd lost him there. I waved my hand in front of his face and his lower lip began to tremble. He sucked in a long breath and looked directly into my eyes. "...then the screeching stopped cold."

Charley's eyes were taking on the look of madness, "She crawled slowly out of one of those darkened doorways and into the middle of the alley where she slowly crouched down like she was getting ready to pounce. She was staring directly at me. I couldn't move. I was afraid to move. I felt like a mouse being tested by a hungry cat."

"So, it was a cat?" I asked, "A black cat?"

"No ordinary cat, no sireee..." he corrected. "A cat the size of a carnival pony! Biggest panther I'd ever laid eyes on and black as onyx." He sucked in another breath. "I could see her powerful shoulders twitch a little every time I exhaled. The moonlight reflected off the glossy shine of her sleek black hair. She flipped her tail carelessly to the left and then to the right."

He swallowed hard and continued, "Her eyes were reflecting the light like hundreds of sparkling emeralds… She didn't move for a long time; just kept staring at me."

I noticed Charley was sweating so much that it was now dripping off his chin and onto the table. He took a hanky out of his shirt pocket and wiped it across his forehead once, then folded it and wiped at his chin before returning it to its cubby-hole.

The room didn't feel especially warm to me. I looked to see if anyone else was showing signs of being hot. The room felt eerily distant. No one in the bar was talking. Perhaps they were listening to the story. Yet, no one moved to light a cigarette or to take a swig of their beer. The room looked unreal… staged.

I turned back to Charley and motioned for him to continue. He shook his head and took another rattled breath. "It was like watching a movie in slow motion as she got to her feet. It was hot as hell in that alley. I don't know if the night air had gotten warmer or if I was just hot from my incessant shaking. Gotta tell ya, pal, even my toes were vibrating."

There was a small thread of blood trickling from his right eye and gathering in one of the creases that ran down the side of his nose. I wanted to stop him but couldn't make the words exit my mouth. I felt like I was under his spell.

He shuddered once and gasped, "The air… I couldn't breathe. I was choking and I could feel something being pulled from my chest."

Charley put his hand up to his throat for a moment as if he was reliving it. "I kept thinking to myself, if only I could move my feet and run. I was frozen like a statue to the place where I was. The panther grunted out a couple of breaths… oomph, oomph, oomph, and then she threw her head up and stood on her back legs."

Charley shook his head and began to speak slower, more deliberately, "As she took one step toward me I noticed something happening to her skin, it was changing. It seemed…it looked like it was beginning to liquefy. Every step forward produced more and more of that black inky fluid."

The old storyteller's voice began to crack, "She was a huge beast standing there before me. Almost the size of a bear and then, in the blink of an eye, she morphed into the shape of a woman! I couldn't believe my eyes, she was beautiful!"

My eyes didn't leave the old man for a second, "Did you say... woman?"

I looked around the bar and nobody seemed moved. Not one sound could be heard from the otherwise talkative Burt. Everyone was in the trance, except for me. "What's going on here?" I shouted into the muted silence. "What is this all about?" The room seemed to be closing in around me.

I turned back around to Charley who was beginning to look very gray in the dim light of the room. I started to lean forward to speak to him when he began again. "She was a raven-haired beauty," he whispered as if he could see her standing right behind me. "Her skin was as white as alabaster; opalescent and almost translucent it was."

"I knew better than to touch her, yet my hand was reaching out for her in spite of it. She was so near that I could hear her panting and feel her exotic breath on me." Charley's hand was now at his chest and he was fingering the collar of his shirt. The sweat was still dripping from his chin onto his hand and running down his elbow and onto the tabletop.

"She danced... for me." He choked the words out. "It felt good... whatever she was doing to me there, didn't matter, it felt so good."

"Are you okay, Charley?" I asked him. "Do you need a glass of water?" I turned to see if someone was coming to help. No one moved.

"She danced and danced." Charley was breathing hard. "And she was using me. ME! She was sucking... the life... right out... of me!" The old man's eyes were rolling upwards and his mouth began to contort.

I jumped up and quickly made my way around the bar. I filled a glass with water from the sink for Charley and thought I must be in some sort of dream myself or something out of this world… and then I could hear it; the soft motor breathing of a cat's purr. Not a small house-cat purr… something… larger.

I froze. "Harry? Did you hear that? I asked over my shoulder. "Can anyone hear that?"

No one responded. The mannequins at the bar did not move. I found myself glued to the floor in front of the table as Charley stood up. "Charley?" I asked. "Sit down, take a sip of this and sit back down. You don't look so good."

The storyteller was getting paler and his face was becoming more drawn by the second. He was beginning to drool.

He coughed once more and wiped his chin with his hand again. "I heard music." He said. "Some sort of eerie low pipe sound and drumming. The drums were beating faster and then faster again. Her body was limber and bending into positions I didn't think the human body could conform to, but I don't think she WAS human. Not human at all."

His breathing was becoming labored. "The shadows seem to be dancing with her there in the alleyway. All the while, she was throwing her head back and writhing like a voodoo priestess before a sacrificial fire. I remember thinking that I might be the sacrifice that night, but she no longer seemed to even notice me there. She had what she came for."

He turned and looked one more time into my eyes before collapsing onto the bar-room floor.

The vacuum in the room seemed to be pulling at my chest and was becoming unbearable and then, at once, released me. The overhead lights flickered. Suddenly the tavern was alive again.

The lights flickered once more and Burt's engine roared to life. "Panthers don't come to the city!" he preached, "They keep to themselves up there in the hills; nothing down here for them, if they know what's good for them."

Marv and Al rose from their stools. Marv took his dollar bill off the bar leaving the change for Harry. "See ya, old man.

Time to go… morning comes early!" Al attempted a small wave and turned to follow his roommate out the door.

"SOMEONE HELP ME!" I shouted. Charley's eyes rolled under the loose skin of his eyes before they opened and focused on something behind me.

Harry was yelling into the phone on the back counter near the cash register. "Might be a heart-attack, hurry!" then slammed the phone back onto its cradle.

Charley coughed a couple of times and then his eyes fixed in their sockets. He was gone.

I stood up holding on to the back of my chair for support. It felt like my own legs had gone to rubber. "He's gone, Harry." I turned to see Harry's face a little paler; his eyes had that hint of craziness behind them.

Harry turned his head toward the spot where Tess had been sitting. She was nowhere in sight. Her drink sat on the bar untouched and there wasn't even the slightest hint that she'd ever been there.

"Where is she?" I asked. "Where did she go?"

"Who?" Harry answered looking blank.

"Tess. Did she leave?" I inquired again.

"I don't know no Tess." Harry answered plainly. He had the look of shell-shock all over him. "There wasn't no girl here."

"Sure there was. She sat right here and this is her drink…" I insisted.

"No!" Harry screamed into my face. "NO GIRL!"

I could hear the sirens approaching in the distance. It wouldn't be long and the bar would be a bee-hive of questions.

"Harry… I saw her..." I whispered back to him, trying to make sense of all of this. "She was sitting right here… a dark haired woman, ivory skin, beautiful green eyes, long legs…"

Just then I saw it move, in the shadows near the back door; a large black cat running into the alleyway.

Three Months Later

"Hey Harry! Nice evening!" I greeted him as I stumbled through the door. "Marv... Al... How's everyone doing tonight?"

Al nodded and Marv beamed his yellow smile while asking Harry to set one up for me.

"Thanks Marv." I stammered. I was already three sheets in the wind by this time every night. This would be my last stop before I'd have to find a place to park myself and sleep it off.

Burt was expounding on the right to bear arms and how we needed to protect ourselves from E.T.'s because the government wasn't doing nothin' about 'em. "As a matter of fact, they are giving them food and shelter in exchange for uranium!" he quipped.

I took my shot of whiskey and beer chaser over to the back table and sat myself down in Charley's old seat. It was mine now. I was the storyteller.

I let my chin fall to my chest and let out a big sigh. It was almost time to close and I needed to get out back and dig for a bag of garbage to lay my head on.

I remember mumbling something to myself about black cats…

THE WEDDING BED

He could taste the dirt in his mouth. It was packed into his throat so he could not cry out. The weight of the earth was crushing him.

"Devon!"

He could hear his name being called to him from… somewhere above him. Her voice was distant but familiar. He was not yet fully awake and his mind kept drifting to another time, another place. Her face, he could see her face…

It was late September, 1928 and the moon was full. The streets were illuminated by the moonlight. Devon was walking with his new bride. The day had been glorious. She was still dressed in her tea-length ivory dress, he in his tux. They made a handsome couple. They were young and they were in love.

She stopped and stood looking up at him. She could have been an angel standing there, the only thing missing were her wings, but she would not need them. She smiled and stroked his cheek lightly. He could feel the slightest quivering of her hand as she brushed it over his skin.

"Is the chill too much?" he asked her.

"No, my love, I am a blushing new bride. My body is alive with the excitement of the day!" she answered him. Her smile was competing with the light of the moon as it lit up her face and surrounded her with an innocent glow.

"Take my hand." he instructed with a renewed enthusiasm. "We are married now and I cannot wait another minute."

Devon had waited for months to marry his true love and then, finally, to make her his eternal wife. "If you cannot walk these two blocks to our home and our wedding bed, then speak up now and I will carry you in my arms!"

She giggled. "I can walk well enough, Devon; please don't exhaust your self. You will need your strength to finish this, so that we can be together, forever."

Devon could hardly resist the desire to throw her to the ground and devour her there. He chose to refrain from his addiction and to wait for the perfect moment to consummate their love. He must focus… first things first!

He pulled her to him and gazed lovingly into her eyes. "My angel" He sighed to her. "Your eyes sparkle like the stars in heaven. He traced her mouth with his fingertips. "Your lips are smooth and supple like the petals of the rose."

Again, she stroked his cheek gently with the back of her hand. He could smell her delicate perfume. She was still trembling so he drew her even closer and continued, "The rose does no justice to the sweet aroma which only you possess. I should drink you slowly like a fine brandy. I will savor its warmth as it enters my throat and close my eyes as it fills me with its intoxicating spell."

"Devon, my dear Devon" she answered him in a soft voice. "Within the hour you will have me. Command the sorceress to release you from this spell and we will continue to our bed."

He put his arm around her shoulder and they continued on toward their new home.

———◆———

He could hear the tearing of the ground above him. He was beginning to realize his fate here. He was buried beneath the weight of the ground. He was buried *alive*?

Devon tried to move his fingers, his toes, to feel for a gap in which he could move and work to free himself. It was of no use; he was packed solidly into this place and could not move.

"Devon! I'm coming, hold on!" he could hear her voice. He tried to answer but to no avail… he was remembering.

———◆———

As the two were making their way up the steps to the door of their 12th Street brownstone they heard a scream and the awful sound of metal twisting and crashing nearby.

Devon sensed the worst. He could see that his bride was moved to help. How very human of her to think she could barter with death.

"Catherine, it's too late, her fate is sealed. Let her be and we will continue with our plans." He spoke to her. "Please! Catherine?"

She could not ignore the screams of pain. She pulled herself away from Devon's arms and ran to the next block.

The woman was lying on the ground before her, torn and broken, barely alive. She realized in an instant that her efforts could not save the woman lying before her.

"Please help me." The woman begged her. "Please. It hurts. I need… I need help. I don't want to die."

"It will be over soon." Catherine whispered under her breath.

Catherine could see the woman's hand shaking as she tried to reach out for her. She was lying in a pool of crimson ribbons. Clearly, it would not take long. Catherine could do nothing.

———◆———

He was becoming more aware now. There was the scraping and beating of the ground above him, yet there was no beating of his heart, no movement at all within his chest.

He wasn't breathing. And, yet, he was aware and alive.

"Who is this woman calling my name?" His thoughts were burning to remember.

———◆———

Devon was standing beside Catherine now and she could see the sweat that was dripping from his brow. He wouldn't be able to control this, she thought. There was too much blood.

Before Catherine was able to stop him, he was already making his way toward the mortally injured woman.

"Please don't." Catherine was moving her mouth to speak but no words came out. "Please, Devon, stop."

It was too late, the bloody scene was too much for him to ignore. He did not have the strength to fight it. He slowly dropped to his knee and picked up the mangled arm of the woman. She was sobbing uncontrollably. Her eyes were wide and had that look of desperation to them. He understood. She was dying. She knew she was dying.

"Don't touch her!" Catherine screamed. "Devon! Do not defile her!"

Devon froze at the command.

"Devon let her go. I will satisfy you, my dear. Please leave her, let her go."

Devon could not control his own instincts as they pulled him down and closer to the dying woman. He closed his eyes and began to lap at the spilled blood like a kitten to a bowl of warm milk.

Catherine could not believe what she was seeing. He would not touch the woman, she was certain. But, his face was covered in the scarlet stain of her blood as he continued to drink from the pool next to her.

———◆———

"Catherine" he thought. It came to him with a jolt. "Her name is Catherine."

He was beginning to remember her.

She was tall and lean. Her hands were delicate and her fingers long; she would rake them through his hair and caress his face. She was soft to the touch, skin of silk, the color of buttermilk, and her cheeks and mouth blushed with a hint of coral.

Her mouth, relaxed in a permanent sensual pout, coaxing him to kiss her and surrender himself, body and… soul.

———◆———

"You there!" came a harsh shout from behind her. "Stop what you're doing! Stop him!"

He was discovered. They would not forgive this… this spectacle of depravity. She did what she knew she must do and ran away from the ghoulish display and the events she knew would follow.

Several men were wrestling Devon to the ground and held him down. Devon looked for Catherine but knew in his heart she had gone. She had to go. She had to survive. He looked up at the streetlamp and suddenly everything went dark.

Catherine watched from the window as they carried his limp body away and loaded him onto the bed of a truck. Some of the men now had shovels and pick-axes with them. She knew what they intended. All she could do now was to wait.

———◆———

"Catherine. My sweet Catherine." Devon could not understand the events that led him to this. He was certain that he was lying in his grave, but why?

Again, his mind took him to another time. She was laughing. With her head thrown back and cares tossed aside, she was happy and giggling as he tickled her with a fine peacock feather, tracing the length of her neck.

"I'm yours!" she was nearly in tears from the joy of it. "Take me now, Devon. Take me away with you."

"I will, my love, but after we have taken our earthly vow." He stubbornly replied. "I must have you in *both* worlds!"

They laughed together like two children at play. They were in love.

———◆———

She had to wait one year. He must lie undisturbed for one year. That is what he told her to do in case something like this was to ever happen. And, it had.

It was the anniversary of their wedding day and of that fateful night when they took him and buried him in this unmarked grave. There was no need for a coffin. They were in a hurry to put him in the ground that night, before the sunrise.

She had watched them place him in his bed, a burial unfit for man or god. She wasn't sure which he was; perhaps both. Now she was standing over him, calling out his name, to awaken him from his sleep. "Devon!" she cried out.

———◆———

He could see a hint of light peeking in from above him. As he was struggling to stay awake he noticed an urgency he could not define.

The pain was growing more intense. He could feel the hunger burning inside of him. He must feed or die.

The light was being cast by a flame inside of a glass box which she was now holding out above him. He could feel the earth release him and he tore at the ground to free himself.

Catherine stepped back and waited for him to rise out of the depths and join her. It was not a mortal body she saw lifting from below her. It was more of an apparition, a ghost, the essence of her love – Devon.

Come to me, she beckoned. Come… to… me. She was speaking to him without making a sound.

As Devon was summoned forward from his grave, Catherine untied her cloak and let it fall behind her. He was being carried upon a mist to her side. He could feel her life emanating from her like the rays of a sun in another galaxy. It was calling him to her; light beckoning to the dark.

Standing before him, Catherine had disrobed and was now holding a small dagger in her hand. With the blade she skillfully cut a small gash into one side of her neck, careful to cut the vein and not the artery. It was important that she bleed out slowly, to stay alive until it was done. The blood was winding lazily from her wound and lacing delicately around her neck as she took a step toward him.

Devon could smell the sweet earthy musk of her blood and pulled her to him. Their lips touched and he could taste her on his tongue.

They fell to the ground together in a frenzy of lust that could not be constrained. He entered upon her there and felt the rush of life that now enveloped his senses. She held him to her and thrust once more against him. It was almost finished.

"You must consume me here, Devon. Now." she whispered to him softly. "You must taste my blood and drink life so you will not perish."

He could not speak. His actions were no longer his own, but that of consuming desire.

He slowly lifted her chin. Devon could smell the scent of her everywhere at once, both the metallic aroma of venous blood and the richer heavier scented blood pumping just below it.

He did what he needed to; he ripped at her throat with his teeth until he could feel the artery. The cord was thick and throbbing with its rich sustenance. He bit again. Catherine released a moan from beneath her breast. She was almost spent. He would have to hurry.

One more time he bit into the rubbery tube and finally severed it. The blood was pulsating into his mouth and he swallowed hard. It was not the sweet taste of death he held in his mouth but the coppery metallic taste of life. Her life.

Devon drank from her throughout the night. Catherine had separated from her mortal body before the sunrise. She lay pale and limp in his arms. His bride had satisfied him in life… and in death.

There was one more task at hand.

Devon placed the body of his bride next to his own, in the grave. There, the two mortal bodies will remain, in the grave that had now become their wedding bed.

Devon stood over the freshly turned soil that was now packed down solidly, and held out his hand. Catherine, resplendent in her immortal glow, reached out and took it. Together they walked away into the night, and into their eternity.

AURALI

The sound was heavy coming from the room inside. The boom-boom of the bass could be felt in the ground outside the gates. *Tsssk Tsssk, Clap Boom, Clap Clap* – The rhythm was hypnotic and calling us forward to come in and join the orgy on the dance-floor.

"I need to see some I.D." said the burly Latino bouncer standing at the gate. His hair was the color of night and so greasy that it reflected the lights that bounced around with the music. "I.D. Sweetie or move aside."

I pulled my drivers license out of my back pocket and handed it to him. He shone his pen-light on the I.D. and then at my face. "Ah, okay – pretty girl." He snickered and leered, "Remember what your mommy told you, don't talk to strangers!"

Katie was right behind me and letting the music flood her senses to the point that I thought I was going to have to slap her to bring her back to reality. Twenty one years old and surviving on the radiance of life. I miss the days before... I miss the normalcy of being human.

Katie was a tall girl, all legs and model-thin. I hated standing next to her; it made me feel like an over-developed third grader. That's right. She might have the statuesque beauty of a goddess, but truth was - she had no shape. I was doubly blessed in that area. I was petite but loaded up front where it counts.

"Just look at me." She would whine. "I have no boobies and my two front teeth are crooked." (Like anyone would notice the slight imperfection of her two front teeth.)

Katie was a society-girl, as they call girls like her; always dressed and made-up as if every moment was a red carpet opportunity.

Her fiery red hair coiled and curled naturally and cascaded down her back like a bloody water fall. She moved like a gazelle, effortless and graceful. It was easy to see how she could cut through the thickness of the room like a razor sharp knife without anyone ever feeling the slices left in her wake.

I, on the other hand, stood five foot - four and three-fourths inches tall and I had to work every inch of it to get from point A to point B. My hips balanced my ample bosom and when I entered a room you could feel the furniture huddle closer to the walls to avoid the inevitable impact with my hips. Watching me move through the room was akin to observing a macabre pinball game.

My mother blessed me with her high cheek bones and perfectly arched eye-brows. They accented the turquoise hue of my eyes and animated my expression to the point where I sometimes needed no words. All that and framed by a halo of honey blonde hair that resembled two soft angel hands cupping my face.

I may not have had the moves or the stature of Katie Welch but once I got your attention I could hold on to it for as long as I liked. And now, I liked it - a lot.

I half-heartedly scanned the bodies in the room before tugging Katie toward the bar. "I'm going to run a tab, Kate – what do you want?" I asked as I placed my own order, rum and coke, twist of lime, and handed the bartender my credit card.

"Just soda for me, I don't want this to end before it's begun." She tossed her hair back like the diva she pretended to be.

"Okay, then, just a soda for my friend." I smiled at the girl making our drinks. She didn't seem very interested in what she was doing; more mechanical, programmed, or robotic in her movements. She glanced up at me for a moment before taking the card and, without so much as a twitch in her expression, scanned the card and gave it back to me.

Yellow, I thought to myself and dismissed it. I scanned the room one more time as Katie and I stood unnoticed.

Hmmm, all the choices. I always have to choose, one or the other – can't we just have them all?

Katie was feeling the hypnotic flow of the room. A steady boom da-boom was permeating from the walls and the dance floor, while the screeching sound of a female vocalist was hanging high on the rafters. *Take me… let's do it again… ahhhh! Taste me… I give you my sin… give you my sin… again and again…* came her high octave rants.

Jeez, to think they actually lose themselves to this; music and the mortal ear – a portal to the orgasmic brain. Whatever.

"Go ahead, Katie." I called out to her. "Go on and dance if you want, get it out of your system. I'll wait up here."

The dance floor was flooded in an array of colors as the lights turned and flashed with the beat of the music. As you moved toward the center of the room you found yourself descending onto the dance-floor, like a sunken living room of sorts. It made it easy, from my perspective, to get a real sense of the energy as it rose above the heads of the dancers. All the bumping and grinding created wave after wave of the sweet smell of life; they, in their ecstasy, and soon – me in mine.

He was watching me from across the dance floor as he stood next to the railing that fenced the voyeurs off from the exhibitionists. I acted as if I hadn't noticed and followed his every movement as he made his way closer.

"May I buy you another?" he nodded toward my now empty glass.

"Why would you want to buy me a drink?" I answered. "Do I still look thirsty? Or is this an attempt at breaking-the-ice?"

"I just wanted to…" he stammered at the unexpected challenge. "I was watching you from across the room. You were standing here alone and I'm not here with anyone…"

"So you thought I looked – lonely?" I was toying with him like a cat with a mouse.

"No. Not at all…" I could tell he was losing his balance.

"It's okay," I assured him with a coy smile. "My name is CeeCee." I extended my hand for a proper shake and instead he gently lifted it to his lips, hesitating long enough for me to feel the warmth of his breath before the softness of his kiss.

"Levi." He didn't say anything else and seemed to be inspecting the top of my hand.

Perhaps he was looking for evidence of a reaction from his unexpected chivalry. Instead, I hadn't reacted at all. There was no offer of my hand other than for a cordial shake and yet I didn't pull away. I allowed it to flow.

"Levi, like the jeans?" His focus on my hand had been broken. He smiled and then slowly looked up once again meeting my eyes with his own. "Nice to meet you, Levi." I said with a grin.

"Let's start over, shall we? Hello, I noticed you from across the room. My name is Levi Thornton." He extended his hand for that cordial shake now.

I extended my hand again, this time to clasp his, and replied, "CeeCee Donovan, I'm glad to make your acquaintance." I tried to sound proper but found myself giggling at the absurdity of it. "Yes, Levi, I will have that drink if it's still being offered."

"Of course." With that he propped his elbow out for me to take it as he escorted me to the bar. "What would you like?"

"I'm having rum and coke, slice of lime, and *you*." I held him in my gaze and waited for a reply.

"Rum and coke with a twist of lime, please." He ordered to the bartender. I watched as she turned and prepared the cocktail without hesitation and without emotion. That's it! She shows absolutely no emotion, definitely yellow.

Levi put a ten-dollar bill on the bar and waved for her to keep the change. That's quite a tip, I thought to myself.

"I've never been to something like this." He finally spoke. "It's really not my kind of place."

"What is… your kind of place?" I asked.

"Well, I'm more of a movie kind of guy; cocktails under the moon at a quaint little café to cap off a night at the theater." He leaned in toward me and it looked as if he were trying to savor my perfume, except I wasn't wearing any.

I could sense the uneasiness in him now. It was like a deer that was grazing in the middle of the field suddenly responding to the subtle scent of the wolf.

"Excuse me. Sorry." It was Kyle and he was tapping Levi on the shoulder. "CeeCee, may I speak with you?"

Levi looked a bit nervous. I could smell the fear. He took his cell-phone from the pocket of his jacket. "I have to take this call. Please excuse me." With that he vanished toward the exit door.

Well, that was odd. I began to wonder if it was my breath or perhaps something worse… and then I just laughed to myself.

"CeeCee, we never go one-on-one with red, you promised." He scolded, "Even if he is a newbie."

"Kyle!" It was Katie and she looked frighteningly tall with her arms stretched over her head waving about. "CeeCee! Elliot is here!" Sure enough he was. Elliot Wagner, the only guy I know who could wear eye-makeup better than any woman could.

"Hello. Elliot." I said coldly.

"Now, you're not still mad about that little incident with Kyle, are you?" He smiled even more coyly than I could ever hope to… bitch.

I had a horrible school-girl crush on Kyle for most of elementary, middle school and high school. Everyone knew Elliot was 'out' but no-one expected to see him walk in to Arlington High School, hand-in-hand with Kyle that day; the day my life changed forever.

"CeeCee! Kyle is playing tonight, are you going?" It was Cameron and Jena, the gossip queens of Arlington Heights. We were in our senior year and counting down the days until we were free of the bondage of parental controls.

Kyle Manning was the cutest boy in Arlington Heights as far as I was concerned. His dreamy blue eyes against his perfectly tanned skin gave every girl a shiver up her spine when their eyes would meet. Kyle was mysterious and shy which made him all the more adorable. He was one of the rotating starting pitchers for the Arlington Badgers.

Of all the animals that could be chosen to represent our fine school, why did the fore-fathers choose badgers? They could have picked panthers or bulldogs and it would have conjured up a nicer image... but badgers? A weasel? That's what it really is, and a close cousin to the skunk. The only redeeming quality in the name is that the badger will take on, and usually win, a fight with wolves, coyotes and even bears. You just don't mess around with the badger.

Well, I suppose Kyle was a lot like a badger in some respects. He was a loner most of the time, when he wanted socializing he kept to a few close friends, and when you threatened him or one of his friends he was the first to fight. Once he got hold of you, there wasn't much that could pull him off.

He was fiercely loyal. The only child of an older couple, he didn't have anyone to truly bond with except his friends. They really were his extended family; his brothers.

The only girl to ever be accepted into the boy's club was me. I wasn't a threat to them like other girls who giggled and wanted to throw kisses. I was one of them. I got dirty. I was always good for two or three home runs in the neighborhood kick-ball games as well as the impromptu baseball games we played in the field behind Jason Huffington's house.

I don't know if Kyle knew just how much I liked him. When we were together it was more like admiration. I not only wanted to be with him, I wanted to be him. It was a strange love.

Yes, I do believe he loved me in some way and he knew I loved him – but, it never occurred to him that I was interested in him romantically. We just fit.

Elliot was a diva. His parents and Kyle's parents were best of friends. Kyle never thought badly of Elliot, and it was this acceptance that paved the way for Elliot in school. Everyone wanted to be friends with Kyle, so everyone was friends with Elliot - everyone but me.

There always had been a possessive quality there that I couldn't put my finger on. And, every time Kyle was team captain and got to pick first, he would grabbed my arm and call out "CeeCee!" I was always the first pick which infuriated Elliot.

I had gotten up that morning like any other morning; running late. I washed my face, brushed my teeth and then my hair, carefully pulling it into a low ponytail that would hang over my right shoulder. Not a high in the middle of the head, swishy bouncy cheerleader kind of ponytail. This was a get it out of your face and contained so you can put your baseball cap on later with ease kind of ponytail.

I thought maybe one day Kyle would take notice of me as a girl. I had no idea.

Lynette, Miranda and I were standing near the school's east entrance when Lynette's mouth fell open. Miranda and I were turning in the direction Lyn was looking when Miranda announced the couple, arm and arm, entering through the doorway. "Elliot! Kyle?"

Then the eyes all turned to me. "Kyle?" I said in a voice I didn't recognize as my own. Kyle looked directly into my eyes. There was a contempt there I had never seen before. The confusion made my head spin and I quickly reached for the wall to steady myself.

Miranda was trying hard to make the situation less shocking. "Hey Elliot, do you need a ride to the game tonight?

"You know I'm not interested in games involving balls." He answered with a coy smirk.

"Depends on the game." Miranda whispered to me.

"Depends on whose balls." Lynette corrected.

My gut felt empty and my mind was overflowing with emotion. All my dreams shattered. And, who was this guy standing in front of me? This isn't my Kyle. What did he do with *my* Kyle.

The rest of the day was a blur. The only time my vision was 20/20 was when I saw the two of them standing together, hand-in-hand, in the hallway between classes. I just couldn't make myself understand. And the oddest thing about all of this was how absolutely fine this was with everyone else. Was I the only one who didn't know? Was I so in love that it blinded me to who he really was?

I didn't go to the game that night, or any night after that. The depression and loneliness I felt was heavy and seemed to pull the life right out of me. I just didn't care any more…about anything.

"You need to cheer up, CeeCee." It was Katie Welch and she was actually talking to me as if she cared.

"Katie?" I answered. "Are you talking to me?"

"Darling, everyone is sick of watching you waste away. You've been walking around in a dazed funk for too long now." She WAS talking to me. "I'll pick you up at 10:00 tonight. It's time you move on and enjoy life. And you are going to meet some very interesting people who, I assure you, will make all your troubles go away. "

"No. I mean, I really appreciate it, Katie…" I was trying hard to find an excuse but nothing was coming to mind. It was as if she were blocking my thoughts.

"Ten O'clock." She said again with a knowing smile. "Jeans and T-shirt are fine. It's casual dress." With that she turned and threw me a backwards wave.

She didn't wait for my response. Oddly, I knew I was going out with Katie Welch and I knew I was going to meet some very interesting people.

━━━◆━━━

Katie pulled up into the driveway in her yellow Porsche 911 Turbo and revved the motor. Don't honk, I thought to myself as I scurried out the door and waved to get her attention before she did anything else to bring attention to herself and to me.

I snuck out of the house to avoid a lot of questions from my mom about my sudden interest in Katie Welch and her group of friends. It was out of character for me - though, for the past month or so I had forgotten who I was and had no idea who I was becoming. This seemed as good a place as any to begin. I was redefining CeeCee Donovan. It was time to let go of the past and embrace the future…with Katie and her friends…what *was* I doing?

"Get in; we don't want to be late!" She called out to me.

I opened the door and eased myself downward into the most awesome ride I'd ever been in. The car itself, seem to mold to our bodies. I could feel the power. Maybe this was going to be fun after all.

Katie put the car in reverse and did a half donut spin out of the driveway before locking it in drive and kicking it into warp-speed. It was exciting and breath-taking. I loved the flash, the speed and the exhilaration of just being with Katie. She possessed energy about her that I couldn't define but I knew I wanted to taste.

We left the familiar roads of town and headed down the winding roads of country living. The sky above us was black and filled with stars. The moon was just beginning to burn bright as it rose over the horizon; a full moon that made the evening all the more surreal.

Soon we were pulling off the main road and onto a long narrow drive that took us past an opulent old estate and onward to what is known as a pole barn. It was a huge out-building wrapped in fabricated metal. I could hear the sound of techno-music coming from inside the building and there were cars parked everywhere. I would have guessed this to be a new-wave ho-down.

Katie stood out even in blue jeans. Her goddess-like beauty was undeniable. Her jeans fit like a second skin. But, true to her superior fashion sense, she didn't top it off with a simple tee. Her upper body was wrapped in a sheer body hugging leotard. Her tiny breasts were perfectly hidden behind the metallic sheen of the fabric.

"Come on CeeCee!" Katie smiled her big trade-mark smile. "You are going to feel much better once we get inside!"

We entered into a cavernous room with lights flashing everywhere and in every color of the spectrum. Some of the revelers were wearing lighted headbands or waving glowing batons in the air. Bodies were bouncing in unison and the look of sheer ecstasy on their faces was inviting.

The music slowed down. Was that Donna Summer singing? *Ooooh, it's so good, it's so good, its soooo good...* The bodies on the dance floor were swaying with hands above their heads in sync with the rhythm of the music and something else, though I couldn't quite put my finger on it.

"Is this a *RAVE*?" I asked. My first RAVE. Oh my, this was different!

"Yes, I guess you could say that." Katie answered. "But not like the Raves you've heard tell of, I'm sure."

That was like Katie, always thinking of herself as better than the usual. Even here, down to the party going on in front of me, always bigger and better. But, I had to admit, this place was full of energy and full of life.

"Come on, CeeCee, let's dance!" Katie took my arm and pulled me into the center of the room where the music filled my head and took me away, far-far away, from the outside world. I was floating away from the sadness and the gloom. I was being whisked away and into something far more sublime than I had ever imagined possible.

Katie leaned in close to me and spoke clearly and directly, "The music will stop in a moment and when it does, lift your arms and breathe deep, inhale the energy in the room. It's hypnotic!"

"What am I inhaling?" I was a little frightened by this. "No drugs, please. I don't do drugs or get high or …."

"Relax CeeCee." She said reassuringly. "It's nothing like that. It's pure energy. Just catch your breath and breath it all in. It's a very organic."

I was still apprehensive about this impending moment of shared inhalation. And, without warning, the music stopped. There was an instant and deafening silence, except for the sound of one big unified breath being taken in by crowd.

Inhale. Exhale. Inhale deeper. Exhale.

The feeling was euphoric. I was instantly filled with light. For that one brief moment I felt as if I could open my arms and fly high around the room and see the individual faces of those below. There was a connection firing within the room. You could smell it…it was a little like the ozone smell of electrical currents or the smell you sense before a lightening storm.

The hair on my arms and the back of my neck stood up and my skin had a gentle crawling sensation within it. The blood rushed up to my face and back down. There was a feeling in my gut like being on a roller-coaster ride, weightless, rushing, that feeling of having your stomach taken away after reaching the top and falling fast. Free.

Within seconds the music started again. A group sigh came over the room. The faces of those around me were frozen in a trance-like expression. But everyone was smiling. The build-up of energy was beginning again.

"Well? Did you like it?" Katie was thrilled and seemed to enjoy my newfound experience even more than I did.

"Actually, that was pretty awesome." I replied. "What happened?"

"Come with me, CeeCee," she smiled like a proud big sister telling her younger sister a fantastic secret. "We need to get up there!" She was pointing to a loft area in the back of the building where people were lined up and watching the room below. Again, those silly smiles…and I was wearing one too.

We made our way past so many people I lost count. As we made our way through, I noticed that everyone was touching someone else and sometimes there was a chain of hands holding hands and shoulders touching. As Katie passed through the crowd the people closest to her would touch her arm or shoulder and say hello.

It seemed that everyone here knew everyone else. No one touched me, with the exception of Katie who was now leading me by the hand to the ladder ascending to the loft.

Once I got above the crowd I could see it. Floating above the heads of the dancing throng was a misty cloud-like substance. It was glowing dimly, but glowing never-the-less, I was sure of it. And as the music got faster and faster, and the beat more intense, the mist above the crowd began to take on colors. Dusty rose, muted powder blues, shaded mossy greens…must be the lights.

Katie was now standing behind me and holding me close. Before I could say anything she whispered, "That is the aura building inside the room. Everyone has a different color and they mix and mingle creating a beautiful flow of light and energy. It's beautiful, don't you think?

"Yes, it is beautiful." I echoed.

"Ok. It's time to get back down on the dance floor. I don't want to miss the next release and it will be too intense for you up here." Katie was full of the life that I had lost the day I lost Kyle…to Elliot. Funny, it didn't seem to matter now.

The party went on until just before dawn. Katie didn't say anything as she drove me home. I wasn't in the mood for talking either. I was trying to hold on to that feeling of intensity I had been experiencing all night long. It was slowly fading.

I managed to get up to my bedroom before my parents woke up and found me missing. All I could feel was the full exhaustion of a night well spent; remembering the build up of the dance, the rush of the inhale, the prickly sensations all over my body, and the cool refreshed feeling after.

That day at school I felt different, alive and totally aware. I never noticed how loud the ticking of the classroom clock was. Tick, tick, tick…it counted off the seconds. It was distracting to say the least.

And, when Mrs. Murdock wrote on the black-board I could hear the chalk as it glided across the surface. When the chalk caught and made that screech sound I thought my brain would explode. What was going on?

Everything that day was amplified – the color of the sky, the smell of the pizza in the cafeteria, the feel of a drop of sweat as it traced a path from under my arm - down my side - tickling me until I couldn't stand it any more.

"Katie!" I shouted over to her as she was getting into her car. She waited for me to approach her. There was that mega-watt smile again. "What happened last night? I think I'm still…high…from whatever it was we were inhaling last night. Are you sure it wasn't some kind of a drug?"

She laughed and then looked deeply into my eyes. Now that she had my attention she spoke, "I told you. There were no drugs at that party."

"Well, something was slipped in without your knowing then." I argued. "My senses are so heightened that it's putting my nerves on edge!"

"Not a drug, CeeCee; *aura*. You inhaled life-energy," she corrected. "It's amazing isn't it? You'll get use to it."

"There isn't anything to get *use* to." I was getting more agitated.

Katie reached over with her hand and the current shot through me like I had been touched by a live wire; just like it felt when I was shocked by the old toaster we use to have. Like the feel of one of those joy buzzers we had as kids. Like a surge of adrenaline after hitting a grand-slam… "Wha…" I stuttered before I could get the word out. A complete feeling of rightness flooded my senses and before I knew it, everything was calm. "What… why…how?"

"CeeCee, are you feeling better now?" she asked, though I was sure she already knew the answer. "There is another party tonight but it's a smaller gathering. Do you want to go?"

"I don't know, Katie, tomorrow is Friday and I have an exam in World Lit." I stated with no real conviction.

"CeeCee, you will be just fine tomorrow. You'll see." She smiled and winked at me as if she knew I had no choice. "I'll pick you up around 10:00 again. Just like last night. Oh, and this time I won't honk or rev the motor. I know you don't want your parents to ask a lot of questions about whom you're with and where you're going."

Damn! Was she reading my mind now?

———◆———

I put on my cream colored jeans and cocoa halter-top and pulled my hair back into a French twist and topped it all off with a pretty coral colored hair-comb. And, for the first time, I was actually wearing a sheer lip gloss and mascara to show off my eyes.

I must be out of my mind, I thought to myself as I carried my mothers brown and cream colored wedge shoes with me to the door. I didn't own a single pair of dressy shoes, only flip-flops and sneakers.

What was I doing? Who was I? Everything I thought I understood about myself, my life, my future was strangely lost to me now. What I did know was I had this insatiable craving for... whatever it was that filled the room at that party!

I could hear the Porsche make its way up the road to our house. Katie took her foot off the gas and let the car coast on its own to the driveway. Alive; that's all I could say to describe this awesome feeling I was having as I ran to the car door, opened it and slid into its soft leather seats.

"CeeCee, you look amazing!" Katie gasped in astonishment. "You look like a completely different person, like a new woman! Let's go show you off, shall we?"

All I could summon was a delightful laugh. I am different. I'm happy. I'm alive. And, I am a woman!

———◆———

We parked the car a few houses down from our destination. The house was dark. I would have assumed the owners had gone to bed hours ago. There didn't seem to be anything going on inside the ranch-style home.

Katie put her hand over mine as we made our way to the front door. The door was not locked and before I could put up an argument we were inside. I could hear the music playing from below us in the basement as she led me down the stairs into a finished area the size of the house itself.

I was immediately greeted by an older couple who introduced themselves graciously. "Hello CeeCee and welcome to our home. We are so pleased you could make it. I'm Peter and this is my wife, Nora."

Nora nodded as she handed me a glass of what turned out to be plain ol' party-punch. "We don't drink alcohol here, CeeCee. It interferes with the experience." She smiled sweetly.

My god, she could be my mother! I thought to myself. She could be someone's mother from school...

"Come with me, dear. I want to introduce you to the others." She reached out and took my hand from Katie's and I followed.

"This is Alaina and Alexa. They are sisters." She began. One looked identical to the other, twins, and they were sitting so close together that it was difficult to see where one of them ended and the other began.

"Namaste'" they spoke in unison.

Over here we have Cara, Vince and Robby… the greetings came out in perfect harmony. Cara was playfully twisting Robby's hair in her fingers as he and Vince were engaging in a game of thumb-war.

"And over here we have two newcomers, Hailey and Monica." Nora said as she threw Katie a concerned look.

Newcomers? Is this a club? Or a cult? I was beginning to feel the nervousness start in my stomach.

"Its okay, CeeCee." I heard Katie whisper from behind me.

Before I could turn around the lights went off. The room was totally black. The music stopped. I could feel the scream forming in my throat but before it could be released, Katie took my hand. "Shhhh." She reassured. "Just listen."

Breathing. The breathing was in sync; in and out, in and out... Easy breaths... Flowing...

I could hear the distant beat of music as it was slowly building in volume. The breathing kept time. I was listening and participating in this crazy ritual. And it felt relaxing, it felt good, it felt surreal.

Louder and louder the music came; techno music again. I noticed a small light flicker in the corner and it grew into a perfect electric blue outline of the room. Neon, it was a neon light and everything below it was illuminated in an eerie glow.

Everyone was moving closer in the center of the room. Hailey and Monica were in the middle standing back to back. Hailey seemed to relax into it but Monica appeared very frightened. I could see something like steam emanating from their bodies. The steam-like mist was a soft powdery lilac color against the gray white mist coming off of everyone else.

The bodies swayed and bobbed to the beat of the drums and bass, including mine. I was being swept away by a room full of "feel-good" that couldn't be explained.

After what seemed to be an hour of dancing, the music stopped cold. Something inside of me knew what to do…inhale. Inhale deeply. Keep inhaling.

This continued throughout the night with only a few breaks for a drink of punch to re-hydrate and to just sit and let the feeling flow. I don't remember the drive home. I barely remember my frantic attempt at washing off the makeup and mussing up my hair to give the appearance of just waking up.

And, as the morning rolled by, I noticed that I was not one bit tired! As a matter of fact, I was full of energy. I breezed through the exam in World Lit., knowing without a doubt, I had aced the test.

"Hello, CeeCee." Katie mused as she came up beside me at my locker. "How are you feeling today?"

"Amazing!" I gleamed. "Colors are brighter, my sense of smell is sharper, and the sounds…I can hear everything! Individually!"

"It is pretty cool." She responded knowingly. "Too bad about the girl, though."

"What girl?" I asked.

"One of the girls from the party." she said. "Robbie vouched for the two girls but, as it turns out, he didn't know either of them."

"What?" I asked confused.

"Robby wanted to bring something fresh to the party. He said he knew the girls. When you have these close intimate parties it's best to keep the numbers even and maintain a strict balance. Things can go awry very quickly when there are fewer of us arcing. She replied casually. "You know - the aura? Remember?"

"I'm not sure I *know* anything." I retorted. "What happened to the girl?"

"Arcing can become, uh, rather unstable if you're not careful. With even numbers you can find a partner and balance. With a newbie, what usually happens is we just take enough to exhaust the donor while always acquiring balance; we put something back. But we didn't know Hailey was turning." She explained. "Hailey lied to Robby and told him she had never been to an osmotic orgy. As it turns out, she had, and at some point she turned; we kept feeding her making her more aggressive!

We're guessing that after the party she took her little friend Monica home and decided to pull the rest from her there. So now we have one dead girl and one ravenous Aurali running the streets. Now *we* are at risk!"

"What are you talking about?" I uttered the question slowly to emphasize each word. "Slow down and tell me what the hell is going on. Who are *we*?"

"Come on CeeCee. You've pulled and arced twice now, and quite heavily I might add." She smirked. "Don't try to tell me you don't know what you're doing. You may not know the *what* of it – but you do know the *who*, the *why* and the *how*."

"Okay. Maybe I did agree to go to the parties and maybe I realized at some point that there was something in the air that we were all sharing and making us feel good." I protested. "And

I suspect that I'm one of the *we* you're referring to, along with yourself that is now at risk. But, I never killed anyone and I don't understand what this has to do with me!"

My emotions were all over the map and I didn't know whether to run or stand fighting…but where was the threat coming from?

"CeeCee, pull yourself together. I'll meet you at the ball-park after school, and then I'll explain everything. Just don't blow your top, girl…r e l a x !

———◆———

I sat on the first row of the five-high bleachers, waiting. I had a lot of questions running through my head competing with the intensity of the greens of the trees against an azure sky and the serenade of a pitch-perfect mockingbird songstress. Had I really never noticed the beauty of the trills and warbles interspersed throughout her song before my awakening? Yes, there were lots of questions.

Did I really want to know? How could I not want this? How could I return to the dark depressing world that was consuming me after losing Kyle?

Kyle. Where was Kyle? Why had everything changed so quickly?

"CeeCee? Are you alright?" It was Katie and she had brought a couple of her friends with her. "You know Destin and Emily." It was a statement, not a question. They thought it would be helpful if they could sit in on our discussion.

"Helpful?" I asked soberly. "Someone is dead and *we* are at *risk*, I just need to understand this aura thing. How does life go from dismal to delightful and then to deadly? What is it that I've succumb to?

Destin spoke first, "We are Aurali, and we exist on – well, the essence of others. We know how to tap into a fountain of youth, a secret that isn't really all that secret, but humans simply wrap themselves up in their mythological dogmas and lose their natural... sense of things. We feed on the life-force; energy."

"Please," I pleaded softly, "just explain all of this to me in layman's terms."

Katie responded first, "We are all just electrical currents that must maintain balance to continue living. But, we can recharge by moving and exchanging this energy in what we call arcing. The medium that holds these charges and make them accessible is a gaseous substance called an aura."

"But you have to keep it all balanced – osmosis! It's instinct, really." Emily added. "The ancients in the East and in the Mediterranean have even written it down to preserve the knowledge. You've heard of the Karma-Sutra?"

"Enough" Katie stopped her. "What it really boils down to here is that the body is animated with a powerful spiritual substance called an aura. The practice of soul-breathing has been handed down for centuries."

"I'm not an Aurali. So, why me? Why did you take me to that party?" I was looking at Katie and trying to find answers in her expression.

"Elliot and I are... how do I say this ...competing for survival of our units, our *families*." She tried to look me in the eye when she said it, but couldn't.

"I'm food?" I asked the question to her specifically. "Were you feeding on my soul?"

"That was the intention. You were closing down anyway after losing Kyle to Elliot. I figured that I could feed and you would know some happiness before..." her voice faded away, she couldn't finish the sentence.

"Before I died?" I said it for her. "I'm going to die? Is that what you're saying?"

"No. It's too late for that." She corrected. "You've already turned, CeeCee. You have a zest for survival, for life, that is very strong and I just couldn't deplete you enough on my own.

Elliot was at the party in the barn that night. If he found out you were this vital he would have fought me for you, so we circled around you and balanced the energy with our own. It turned you. It was that or surrender you to Elliot. CeeCee, you will need to maintain the balance now to regenerate and stay alive."

"Are you saying that I have to kill someone else to stay alive?" My head was swimming with the revelation.

"There is no death, really." It was Emily again. Her voice soft and calming, "We have survived for millennia and we'll survive for another millennia – the aura does not die and it does not grow or diminish – it's simply passed along. And, with an increase of Aurali, balance becomes more difficult to attain. Elliot and his unit are very aggressive and they have set out to increase their numbers to increase power. We struggle for balance and it becomes difficult to maintain."

Katie put her hand on top of mine and I withdrew it quickly. "You aren't taking another drop of me!" I exclaimed.

"I can't *take* it. You would have to *give* it – freely." Katie explained. "You are one of us now. What is yours is yours, unless you want to share it."

"So, that night in the barn, I was inhaling souls?" I really needed some clarification.

"Not really souls, auras. You pass this on freely anyway, whether you are an Aurali or just a human, when you hold hands, kiss, hug, or lie very close to someone you care deeply for." Destin said with his gentle tone.

It was starting to make sense now. All the closeness at the parties, the hand holding, the rise of the mist in the room, the color spectrums, the heightened senses, the knowing…

"Why are we in danger now?" I asked. "Isn't she one of us? You said she can't take something from us unless we give it freely."

Destin added, "Hailey is a spawn of Elliot's making and she has pledged her allegiance to his unit. You and Kyle were very strong spirited. Your auras were intense by themselves, but together, you were a beautiful force of energy. Both sides have been watching the two of you for years.

When Elliot was successful at turning Kyle you lost your force density and it left you less protected. It was either take you as our own or surrender you to Elliot. Red would win and we would be consumed and merged into and strengthen his core."

"Did you say that he turned Kyle?" I couldn't listen to any more of this. All I could think about was how much I loved Kyle and he was on Elliot's team; the red team.

"I have to go." I said matter-of-factly. "I have to find Kyle."

Emily stood up and blocked me from moving past her. "You just don't get it, do you?"

"I get that I'm in love with Kyle and always have been and you can't suck that fact out of existence! So move out of my way." I was using my tomboy voice now and I wasn't about to back off.

"His aura is dominant now. Elliot keeps him close and they balance regularly to keep their strength up. You cannot possibly expect to overpower either of them if they are together." She was sweating and I could see the mist rising off of her like steam. She was producing a vivid and intensifying blue. Red…blue…teams…units…competition – is this a battle for survival? The red team against the blue and winner takes all?

I looked down at my own arm and saw the same thing happening to me, a steamy mist rising off of my skin and the feel of electrical currents crawling up my arm. I could see it – the aura – we were all emitting various shades of a blue. And, hadn't I seen the mingling of all the colors of the spectrum that night rising out of the crowd below? What color was Kyle?

"The girl, Hailey, will guard Kyle when Elliot is arcing." Emily stated. "If they share their energy it will make her stronger, because, Kyle has not completely balanced to red yet. He started out a blue just like you, CeeCee. But the last time I saw him he was a redder shade of violet than the time before that."

"Can I help him? Is there any way to save him now?" I wasn't crying outwardly but my insides were flooded with emotions. "I have to try. You understand that, don't you? I have to try."

"It's not that easy, CeeCee." Destin cautioned. "The most experienced Aurali can lose control and a surge can be deadly."

"I have to try," I said, "with or without you."

Destin looked to Emily and raised an eyebrow. "I would do it for you."

Emily smiled. "Well, we need a strategy if we want to do this right. I don't want anyone to get hurt."

"There is another big party planned for tomorrow night and it will be at the Lodge of the Fallen Oaks." Katie said with a nod and then turned to face me. "I need to get you ready and prepare you for what might happen there. You might be Kyle's only salvation. I think you can pull him if you can get him to offer himself to you and to you alone."

Destin and Emily got up and offered me a hug. This time I accepted and I could feel the power of their auras pass into me and mine into them. It was such a wonderful feeling, tingly and breathtaking; balance.

I must be out of my mind. Kyle and I grew up together and were perhaps closer to each other than any of the other kids, but would he trust me now? I always knew I loved him and maybe he felt the same but I never really had the chance to find out. It was just assumed that it would be Kyle and CeeCee, together forever.

I applied my makeup with the ease of an artist at her canvas. Who was this young woman staring back at me now? Would Kyle know me? I had my doubts but this seemed the only way to save him from Elliot and a life-time of being red. I giggled to myself. He hated that color anyway. What was the attraction? How did Elliot get him to connect?

Here I was, standing in front of the mirror, thoroughly amazed at my own transformation. Katie and I had gone shopping earlier and she charged an entire ensemble for me to wear tonight. The dress was thigh high and hung over all the right curves showcasing my figure in ways I'd never imagined. The fabric was something altogether different than anything I had ever seen before. It was a shimmering mesh that changed from silver to every shade of blue depending on the way the light reflected off of it. The shoes were strapped heels that shone a beautiful electric blue. Everything about me was aglow in a radiance of blue light.

The Porsche was making its way up the street and again I heard Katie let off the gas so as not to cause any unnecessary attention. I had to get out of the house unnoticed. I felt like advertising for Neon Spectral Lighting, Inc., but I made it to the car without incident.

"Do you remember everything I told you, CeeCee?" Katie looked over at me with a confident smile and a wink as she reached over to touch my hand.

"Yes. I have it all etched right here," I said as I pointed to my forehead, "and here." as I pointed to my heart.

"Okay then, let's go get your man!" she stated firmly.

"Katie, please stay close to me." I was feeling less sure and the weight of how this could all go wrong was heavy.

"Pay attention, we have to stay together!" It was Destin's calm voice. I looked over my shoulder and saw him standing hand in hand with Emily. They didn't look at all threatening. They were just two young kids in love.

The draw of the music and the energy in the middle of the room was impossible to ignore. Everyone melded into a magnetic flow of bodies moving together in primal rhythm.

"I need some water." I said to Katie. "I feel so dry." Katie left for only a moment and returned with two bottles of water.

"Okay, baby girl." She said as she handed me one of the bottles. "It's show time."

I looked toward the door and saw them walking into the party hand in hand. Elliot and Kyle in the middle of four guys who formed a mini-rumba line as they entered.

I had to stay cool - literally. No room for error here. Stay very - very cool.

The room was electrified with the mix of auras and the rising crescendo of the music. I took a long drink and put my bottle of water down on a random table as I made my way to the highest vantage point; a balcony that framed the entire room. From here I could see everything.

The aural mist was twisting and spiraling above the heads of those on the dance-floor. Some colors were bold and bright while others were much weaker and lighter. You could see the distinction of those who were Aurali and those who were not. Aurali transmitted in strong waves and were moving and entwining faster than the plumes of color released from a mere human. Balance, it was a delicate weave of balance.

I would have to get a fix on Kyle's aura and hold it long enough to pull it away from the others when the music stopped. He would feel it, they said. It would feel different to him than Elliott's pull and so long as Elliott was not aware of my intention he wouldn't be guarded. No, Elliott would be concentrating on a new-comer and pulling from them. This would be my only chance. I had to get it right the first time.

I saw an intense flash of red coming from the left side of the dance floor. Kyle was actually dancing to the music. He looked like a god to me, not a boy on the pitcher's mound, but a young man moving in ways I could never have imagined. I liked it, it was captivating and sexy.

I recognized the face of a girl dancing near him. It was her! Hailey! I could feel my aura lifting from me and I concentrated hard to keep it under control. I needed to send it to Kyle only and take his without anyone noticing the channeling of the arc. I had to do this quickly, before she could figure out what was happening and block it. I had to concentrate on Kyle.

I talked to him in my mind and kept my aura cool. Kyle, I love you. Trust me. It's going to be alright. Let me in Kyle and I'll cool your skin with my breath and take away the madness you've been locked behind. I love you. Can you feel me? I'm all around you and I want to give myself to you. Will you give yourself to me?

I could feel the tingling sensation throughout my body and it was building. I was moving beyond anything I'd ever felt before. I was afraid, yet I was yielding to it. The yen and the yang, the ebb and the flow, the in and the out…I could feel my soul wrapping around his and we swayed together with the music…breathe in; breathe out…mine, yours…

He jerked as if someone had slapped him. Slowly he lifted his eyes and met mine. "Easy Kyle. Trust me and let me guide you darling. Breathe with me…in… out, slowly…focus."

Kyle nodded towards me to let me know he understood. We were communicating with our souls. I could feel the heat of his aura as it began to merge with mine. He was strong and instinctively pulling against me. "No, Kyle. Let go. I love you, trust me and let go so I can cool you. Blue, Kyle – find the blue and focus your energy into it. I'll pull you free."

The beat was getting faster and the guitar rifts were growing more intense. I could see the room was full of the mist and it wouldn't be long now.

"Kyle," I thought to him. "Do you want to give yourself to me?"

I could hear his voice inside of my head, "Yes."

"When the music stops, Kyle – channel everything you have and merge it into me and I will fill you with mine." I instructed him. "I'll catch you baby, I'll balance for us and you'll be free."

Destin and Emily were now standing on either side of me and adding their energy to mine. I could feel Katie standing behind me but I couldn't sense her aura. I knew she would be there when it counted. I relaxed and returned all my attentions on Kyle.

Boom-da-boom, da-boom, boom, boom; the beat was at its apex and ready to release. Then it happened. The music came to an abrupt halt. Kyle's head was thrown back with a jolt of ecstasy and I reached out to pull his aura from him while replacing it with my own. Balance.

The heat was coming on strong. Hailey must have felt the pull and was now struggling to prevent the exchange. I could feel the redness of her aura as it found its way inside of me. I had to focus on Kyle. I was pulling. Pulling! Hailey was trying to block me and just when I thought I couldn't pull any more I saw a spark and a flash of light as Destin's energy knocked Hailey to the floor. Emily grabbed my hand and merged her aura with mine to join in the pull for Kyle. That's when I felt a sudden jolt that broke my connection with Kyle.

Elliott turned around and looked up to face me. Red! I was being swallowed in a vortex of red. Destin immediately focused with Emily on Kyle and began pulling the red aura out as Emily replaced it with blue. I was on my own and embattled with the Red Unit Leader. Elliott was putting up quite a fight.

I could hear him in my head as he spoke to Destin and Emily. "Take him girls." He thought out loud. "I'll gladly make the exchange for CeeCee!"

Yes. I would gladly sacrifice my life for you Kyle, I thought to myself. I could feel myself being drained of my own life energy but I was determined to fight until Kyle was safe.

"CeeCee," the voice, confident and strong, rushed in like a cool wave – it was Katie's voice. "Focus with me. We are going to take Elliott into ourselves."

"NO!" I screamed on the inside.

The red burned hot against the coolness of my soul. I could feel the flash of fire as it passed through every cell of my body. A wicked, angry, sick hotness that felt foreign and forbidden.

Katie put her arms around me and soaked me with her gentle sweetness. Ah, the rush of something that chilled me to the bone; a clean release. I was relaxing in the glow of purest pleasure. The red feeling was gone and all I could feel was… balance.

Kyle? Was he okay?

"CeeCee…" I felt him shimmering and tickling me on the inside. "I love you."

Our eyes locked. He was mine; all mine. "I love you too."

We did it! While Destin and Emily took over and balanced Kyle, Katie and I were able to absorb and deflect the flaming aura of Elliott and destroy it, successfully pulling Elliot into a violet-blue.

"You shorted him out!" Emily explained later. He was now a part of our unit but he still had that rogue quality about him…couldn't completely rid him of those reddish hues.

Katie had planned to be my anchor the whole time. She knew I would need a little extra boost at the climax. Turns out, she *is* pretty awesome!

Kyle was now a sterling steel blue and my love was going to keep it that way.

━━◆━━◆

Kyle and I were accepted to the same university that year and were looking forward to graduating with our degrees in Electrical Engineering! It made sense. We were inseparable now. Katie and the others stayed close by to keep an eye on us. Together we were a force to be reckoned with.

There was no denying that the blue team was a strong entity to deal with and everywhere we went we were sure to strike a balance.

It was near impossible to pull a red into our unit. Elliot was one of the few that it worked on. This one success was enough to convince other reds to move on rather than challenge us and risk a loss.

We were growing up and getting so much better at achieving *BALANCE*. In a room full of dancing bodies, who would be the wiser?

━━◆━━◆

The sound was heavy coming from inside the room. The boom-boom of the bass could be felt in the ground outside the gates. TSSSK TSSSK CLAP BOOM CLAP CLAP – The rhythm was hypnotic and calling us forward to come in and join in the dance-floor orgy.

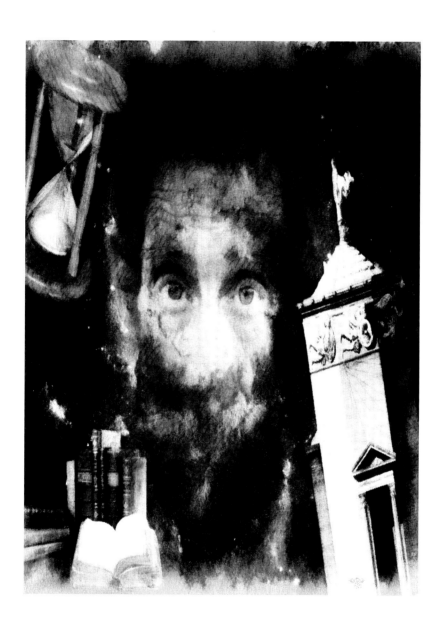

TREASURE OF TIME

I woke up that morning to my Mom's panicked cry for my father; something was wrong. "Roger, get down here, quick! Dad's gone! Dad isn't here, I can't find him anywhere! Roger…"

My brother climbed down out of the bunk above me and the two of us sprinted for the bedroom door.

Dad was rubbing the sleep from his eyes and trying awkwardly not to trip on the rug as he made his way to the stairs.

Mom was on her way up the stairs to come get him. The two of them met in the middle. Mom was sobbing something about Grandpa.

I thought for a moment that he had died in his sleep and that she had made that horrible discovery. Grandpa was living with us now and had a room of his own on the first floor, just off of the den. He had to come to live with us a year after Grandma had passed. His health was steadily getting worse as he grieved the loss of his one and only true love.

Grandpa was older than dirt, as my dad would say, and he spent most of his time with his nose inside a book. Seems he was always reading something. It was something he and Grandma shared a passion for and since her death it was all he did. Maybe he felt closer to her when he was absorbed in a good book. It had to be difficult for him to focus on the print, his eyes were so bad he had to wear those thick magnifying eyeglasses just to see his hand in front of his face much less, the small words typed on a page in a book.

Our Grandpa was a slight man with a round butt that seemed to balance his round belly. His legs were so skinny that Michael and I wondered how long he could stand before they would just snap in two.

"Marky," he'd say to me, "help me to the bathroom, will ya?" I'd help lift him out of his favorite chair and we'd both hobble together, arm in arm, the dozen or so steps it would take to reach the bathroom door.

"Wait for me Marky, would you?" he would ask. "I won't be long."

Jeez, sometimes I would stand there for fifteen minutes or more. I loved my Grandpa. The memories of him as a younger man, carrying me on his shoulders through the crowds at the fair, or taking us to the pond to fish from that old Jonboat, made me smile.

It was always a treat to be with Grandpa, even now. He could tell the best stories. Michael and I would sit entranced for hours listening to his stories about all the places he had visited when he was a "student of the world," as he would tell it.

Michael is my older brother by a year and a half.

He will be a seventh grader this year and I'm in the fifth grade. According to him, I'll be studying many of the same places that Grandpa has told us about. It will be extra special because we have already seen these places in our imaginations.

Grandpa had a way with a story. You could close your eyes and imagine the places he told us about. He would give us *picture perfect* words so we could visualize as we listened. Yep, that's what he called them, "picture perfect words."

But this story trumps them all.

———◆———

Michael looked at me as we were standing frozen at the top of the stairs, "Grandpa?" he mumbled to himself and then turned to me. "Missing?"

"I think that's what she said." I mumbled back.

The two of us bounced down the steps to where Mom and Dad were now holding each other. Mom was crying inconsolably into dad's shoulder.

"Come on, Maggie," he said to her as he slowly escorted her down into the kitchen and helped her to her chair at the table. "Boys, go upstairs and get dressed. We need to look for Grandpa."

As dad was pouring mom a cup of coffee I tapped him on the shoulder and, looking down at my feet, I asked him, "Was Grandpa kidnapped?"

"No. Marky," he assured me. "Must have just taken a walk and Mom's a little upset that he didn't leave us a note or anything. Don't worry about it, get your clothes on and we'll go have a look around."

Gone for a walk? I thought to myself. He can't even get to the bathroom on his own.

I hurried up to our room and found Michael sitting on my bunk lacing up his shoes and looking a bit worried. "What do you think of all this?" I asked him.

"Doesn't look good, Marky." he replied, wiping his nose with the back of his hand. "I just don't know where he would go; where he *could* go. And, it's so cold out there."

I shook my head in agreement. "He couldn't have gone far." I suggested.

"Well, we better hurry." Michael answered. "Mom's going to have a stroke down there worrying about him."

I rushed getting dressed and putting my shoes on and almost forgot to tie the laces. That's all we'd need is me tripping down the steps. I hurried down the stairs and found Dad and Michael already planning where to look.

"I'll take the neighbors to the south and you boys work both sides of the street to the north. Knock on every door and ask the neighbors to take a look around their property and help us look for Grandpa.

"Michael, when you get to Dirk's house, tell him that Grandpa is missing and ask him to call around and see if someone picked him up and took him to the station… or the hospital in Sparta." Dad instructed. With the mention of the hospital Mom threw her head down into her arms on the table and sobbed deeply.

"We'll find him Fran (she was named after Grandpa and Grandma, Frank and Anne). He didn't get far, probably on an adventure somewhere out back." Dad squeezed her shoulder then patted her back nervously.

"Come on boys, let's go." he turned and we all left out the back door.

We lived in a small close-knit community, everyone knew everybody. Every door we knocked on was answered and the neighbors joined us in the search for Grandpa. It didn't take long and word was traveling faster than our feet could carry us. Neighbors were meeting us out in the street to get the particulars.

"Not much to tell," Michael would tell them. "Woke up this morning and he was missing. No note. Just gone, and no sign of where he would be."

Dirk met me at his door just as I was about to knock. "Son, where is your mom?" he asked.

"At the kitchen table crying." was my answer. "We left her at the table, sobbing."

"OK, I'll send Dee down to her to give her some comfort and wait with her until we know something." Dirk was the Chief of Police and Dee was his wife and the town do-gooder. "Don't know what we expect to find, I hope he just forgot himself and fell asleep somewhere warm. We can all be laughing to ourselves tonight at dinner over it." Dirk shook his head and looked down at his feet. I knew he was concerned.

We searched all day and into the late evening. Dirk had called off the search after the sun was down and the sky was black. "We won't see anything out here tonight, even with the flashlights and lanterns. We'll begin searching again at sunrise.

Go home to your families and tell them we'll need every able body out here looking for Mr. Milton… er, Frank… and we'll need those who stay behind to bring refreshments so we can eat and keep our strength up.

Mom's eyes were puffy from crying all day and she looked exhausted when we finally got home. Dad held her for a long time, stroking her hair and letting her cry it out until she couldn't cry anymore. Then he led her upstairs without saying a word to Michael or me. We were old enough to see ourselves to bed.

I stopped at the archway leading into the den and stood staring at Grandpa's chair. Next to his chair was a little table where his reading lamp and books sat. And, as always, perched on top of the books were his 'specs'. They were the thickest glasses I'd ever seen. Specs, that's what he called them, his *specs*.

I rolled it over and over in my mind, how could the old man see, much less walk well enough, to make it very far from the house. Why couldn't we find him? Where could he be?

"Gotta try to get some sleep, Marky," Michael said from behind me. "Morning will come early tomorrow."

"I know, but…" I hesitated. I walked over to Grandpa's chair and sat down. "I can't imagine how he wandered off."

Michael came in and sat down on the sofa to keep me company. "We'll find him…and he'll be okay." His voice was comforting as he tried to offer some assurance and hope.

I picked up the book sitting on top of two others and noticed it was old and worn. It was so weathered that I couldn't find any lettering on the cover at all. "What does Grandpa see in these old books?" I asked.

"I don't know." Michael responded absentmindedly.

I turned the book over in my hand inspecting it carefully. The covering of the book was made of fine brown leather. No writing could be found on the outside or the spine of the book. I opened it and looked for some identification on the inside page and found it blank. I turned the page… blank, and then another… blank, and another… blank, blank, blank!

"Michael." I spoke out, "there isn't any writing in this book."

"What do you mean, no writing? It's a book." He stated mid-yawn.

"Just that; no writing, there is no writing on the cover or inside the book, just blank pages." I said again in disbelief.

Michael let out a huff as he pulled himself up from the sofa and walked over to the chair. "Let me see…" he reached out and took the book from my hands.

After a moment or two inspecting the book inside and out, he looked down at me with his eyes wide and curious. "This is the one he is holding every night before he goes to bed." He stated matter-of-factly. "I know it. I've seen him looking at this very book every night when I come in here to kiss him goodnight."

"What is he reading?" I asked. "Where are the words?"

Without much thought I reached over and picked up Grandpa's magnifying specks and placed them on my face. The room instantly blurred as if someone had covered them in petroleum jelly. I could barely make out the shadow of Michael standing right in front of me, but I could see something written on the leather binding of the book that was balanced in his left hand.

"Let me see that book." I said to him.

Michael let out a deep breath and slowly extended the book towards me. I could see a brown blur coming towards me and I reached out to take the book.

With Grandpa's specs still perched on the bridge of my nose, I slowly looked down at the books worn out cover. I could see something; gold writing…fancy lettering…"The Treasure of Time" I recited out loud.

I slid the glasses off my nose and handed them to Michael. "You can see the writing with these." I told him.

Michael put the glasses on and looked down at the cover of the book.

"How…?" Michael stuttered trying to find the words. "I can see it!" he gasped. Michael opened the book to the first page. "I can read it… all of it…"The Treasure of Time"… there is no date, no author's name, nothing."

"Put it down Michael." I said firmly. "I don't like this. There is something freaky about that book and those… glasses!"

I snatched the book from my brother's hand and put it back on top of the other two on the table. "Now give me those glasses." I ordered, hands shaking.

Michael didn't argue. It was too late in the night to get into a scuttle over a book and goggle-glasses. "Whatever." He shrugged. "I'm going to bed. Are you coming?"

I wasn't sure if I would sleep but I was certain I didn't want to be here in the den with that creepy book and those crazy glasses. I followed my brother up to the bedroom, slipped out of my clothes and into my pajamas and took my place in the bunk below him. It didn't take long before the book and glasses faded away and I was on my way to dreamland.

The morning did come a lot sooner than I expected. I woke to the low voices of several men on the main floor making their plans to continue the search for Grandpa.

A full bladder was suggesting quite firmly that I get up and take care of the problem before doing anything else. I rose from my bunk and rushed to relieve myself. As I stood looking at my own reflection in the mirror over the bathroom sink I remembered those glasses and that odd book. A shiver ran up my back.

I washed my hands and taking the hand-towel with me, I returned to an empty bedroom. Where is Michael? I thought to myself, probably downstairs already, getting something to eat before we head out.

I hurried to get dressed, combed my hair and brushed my teeth so I could help out with the search.

The kitchen table was surrounded by ten or twelve men looking at an old map of the neighborhood. They were plotting out a grid for each of them to cover before lunchtime. But, Michael was nowhere among them.

"Where's Michael?" I asked over my shoulder to my mom, who was busily trying to make another pot of coffee.

"He popped his head in here about a half hour ago and I haven't seen him since." She answered without turning to face me.

I walked toward the den and noticed someone standing near Grandpa's chair. "There you are!" I said as I noticed that Michael was holding that crazy book and donning Grandpa's glasses. He didn't look up right away, just kept on looking at whatever had appeared on the pages before him.

"What are you doing, Michael? I said with some concern. "Was it our imagination last night? Were we just seeing things?" I questioned.

He replied quietly. "It's like last night. Nothing on the book cover or the pages until you put these glasses on, Marky. It's not like there is writing on every page either, just here on the title page and this little rhyme." He paused, "It must be some kind of a trick or something."

"A trick?" I echoed back to him, "Like a magic trick?"

"I don't know yet. There's this strange verse here and I keep reading it over and over and it doesn't make any sense to me." Michael answered.

"Let me see it" I suggested.

Michael withdrew the glasses from his face and handed them to me with the book.

The cover was still blank until you put the glasses on. Then in beautifully ornate golden lettering embossed into the leather, it read: "The Treasure of Time." I opened the cover and read the same on the title page... no author, no publisher, no date. It was just like I remembered it from last night.

However, this time when you turned the page there was a verse written in filigree cursive lettering, like people used back in the quill and ink days.

"What do you think?" Michael asked me as if I could make any sense of this.

"I'm not sure what to think." I replied back to him. "It's really old and I can barely make out the words. Open my eyes…my…ears, hmmm…my mind…"

"I can't make out the next line." I adjusted the glasses and read it again, it looks like it reads: "show me the…hmmm, treasure… I seek to… find? Yeah, I think that's what it says."

We both looked at each other for some clue to understanding the rhyme. I repeated the verse again, "Open my eyes, my ears, and my mind…" to which Michael replied, "Show me the treasure that I seek to find."

We couldn't understand the meaning of it, it was so vague. What treasure?

Michael and I looked at one another and repeated the verse again together, with more conviction, "Open my eyes, my ears, my mind…Show me the treasure I seek to find."

All of the sudden the room began to disappear in a fog. I reached out for my brother's hand as I felt the floor disappear beneath my feet. "Michael!"

———◆———

"I'm right here Marky, grab my hand!" he shouted back to me. We gripped each other tight as the room disappeared from view. As the fog began to fade I opened my eyes to see a look of shock and disbelief on Michael's face. He was looking over his shoulder and all around.

"Michael?" I asked him. "What happened?"

"We aren't in the den anymore." He answered in a whisper. "I don't think we are in the HOUSE anymore."

I slowly began to look around us. We were standing in the middle of a cobblestone street. It was cold early morning, there was a fog hanging low on the street and the sun was just now making its way over the horizon, we could hear bells ringing… church bells?

"Marky, I don't know what just happened, but I think we are in London." He suggested cautiously.

"Like, in London, England?" I asked, trying to clarify what he meant.

"Yep. London, England." Michael assured me. "That, over there, looks like the Clock Tower. I've seen it in pictures."

"Like, in *The Big Ben*?" I couldn't believe what I was hearing, much less that we could be standing somewhere other than in our family den.

"Yeah, Big Ben…" Michael's voice trailed off. "Marky look! Over there! Is that Grandpa?"

Again, I couldn't believe my own eyes. There making his way through the crowded street, was our Grandpa.

"Where are we? How did we get here?" I thought to myself, "And most importantly, where was Grandpa running to, or running from?"

Michael grabbed my arm, "We can't lose him. Come on, follow him!"

"I don't want to follow anybody!" I protested. "I'm freaking out a little bit here! Where is that book? Maybe there is a map or something…"

Michael stopped and turned to me, "I don't have the book. Don't you have it?"

I shook my head and felt my bottom lip begin to tremble. I looked down and saw the book and glasses lying on the ground at our feet. Michael reached down and picked them up, handing them to me. "Michael what's happening?" I stammered.

"I dunno, but we'd better hurry or we'll lose Grandpa!" Michael yelled back over his shoulder as he started jogging in the direction where we last saw him... if it really was him.

I decided to follow rather than stand in the middle of wherever we were...

We ran up to the first turn and realized we had already lost him. A man dressed in white was standing alone on the bustling street corner. He seemed to be selling bags of nuts but no one really stopped or took note of him there.

Michael stopped in front of him and asked, "We are looking for an older man, with trouble walking, and he can't see very well, he would have walked right past you... did you see where he went?"

The peddler looked at us knowingly and told us, "No cripple, but I did see an older gentleman hurrying up that way. He was mumbling something about the time. I figured he was late for an appointment or something. But he did not appear to be crippled and didn't seem to have trouble seeing either."

I looked down to the next corner and to my surprise I could see Grandpa taking directions from a young woman cradling a cat in her arms.

"There he is!" I squealed. "Come on!"

We sprinted up to the next corner. The street sign read, King Charles Street. I caught another glimpse of him as he was weaving in and out of view among the crowds of sightseers.

Whitehall Street, I read from the next street-sign, "We are on Whitehall Street."

"Where did he go? Did you see where he went?" asked Michael trying to catch his breath.

"I lost him." I answered. "The lady was pointing him in this direction, let's keep going."

We were now getting further away from the only point I had recognized; old Big Ben. I wasn't sure of this at all but I had no other choice, really, I had to stay with my brother if I had any hope of making sense of this. After all, we both read the verse together, we both woke up here together, and it seemed to fit that if we were to get home, it would require us *staying* together.

We were running hard for about five minutes and I was panting for air along with my older brother when we finally caught sight of Grandpa again.

"There!" He cried out and pointed up the street. "There he is! Grandpa! Grandpa! Stop!"

I could see him as he stopped and looked around him. "It's us, Grandpa! Wait up!"

Grandpa seemed to look right at us but he didn't see us, or at least that's what I told myself. I was beginning to question a lot of things.

Michael was slowing down but not stopping. I followed but was lagging further behind. We must have run a mile and it didn't seem like we would ever be able to catch up to Grandpa.

"There he is, Markey!" Michael called out again.

We finally reached him at the corner of Richmond Terrace and Whitehall Street. He finally came to a stop. He seemed disoriented looking up and down the streets where they intersected.

I was just about to catch up when I saw Michael place his hand on Grandpa's shoulder. It really is him, I thought to myself.

As I finally reached the two of them I could see that Grandpa was both happy to see us and yet, concerned. "Michael! Markey! What are you two doing here?"

Michael was still trying to catch his breath. I spoke first, "The book, Grandpa… and the glasses…you forgot your glasses." I reached into my pants pocket and withdrew his thick black framed glasses.

"Oh, I see." He looked down at the specs as I held them out to him. "You saw the incantation and read it, didn't you?"

"Incantation?" I spoke loudly. "Like a spell that witches say?" Are you kidding?"

Grandpa shook his head without lifting it to make eye contact with Michael or me. "I'm afraid that is exactly what it is. Magic. It brought you here."

He looked at me and slowly asked, "Did you bring the book?"

"The book sort of came with us. It still wasn't making any sense and the more I thought about it the crazier this whole thing seemed. I truly thought I must be dreaming.

"Well." He said matter-of-factly. "We've managed to meet up here so I suppose we should get to work."

Finally Michael spoke up, "Work? What kind of work? What are you doing here?"

It appeared, at that moment, Michael was more accepting of our little trip to dreamland than I was. While I stood rattled to the bone, he was rather calm and trying to collect information to move forward with. Ah, my older brother, cool as a cucumber in times of distress, whatever.

"We have to find the doorway, boys." He instructed. "We have to find the amulet and the doorway to get back home."

"Amulet?" I questioned.

"Doorway?" Michael added.

"This is where the politicians of London live and play." He told us. He looked across Whitehall Street and nodded, "Downing Street. We are searching for the black door of Downing Street. Then we need to find the side entrance. There we will see the white door hidden between the two buildings. The Witch of Downing Street lives there. She will give us a treasure, an amulet and the incantation to get home."

"Wait a minute." Michael said to him. "The black door, is that the famous 10 Downing Street?"

"Yes it is." Grandpa answered him. "But we don't have business at number Ten Downing Street. We are expected at 9 ¾ Downing Street."

"9 ¾ ?" I laughed. "Is that a real address?"

"You bet it is!" Grandpa put his hands on my shoulders. "Don't worry boys, we'll find it, get what we need, and be home before you're even missed."

"Grandpa!" Michael exclaimed. "You *are* missed! We couldn't find you yesterday. Mom is sick with worry. The town has a search party out looking for you."

"Oh, Michael," I added, "now they are going to be looking for us too! Poor Mom. We gotta get back soon!"

"Let's go find this door, Grandpa." Michael took Grandpa's arm like he usually does at home to help him walk.

"You don't have to help me here, Michael." Grandpa told him, "I'm protected here... for a little while."

"What do you mean protected... for a little while?" Michael asked as we started walking across Whitehall Street.

"The incantation makes us whole again so we can pursue the treasure," but he was beginning to show signs of hobbling again, "but only for a while. I think it's starting to wear off now. We should hurry."

We came to a stop in front of the ominous black gates to Downing Street. Just ahead of us stood a guard, who was now watching us with some interest.

"Back away from the gate sirs." another officer commanded.

Grandpa made his way between us and stepped right up to the black iron gate. With a low and confident tone he spoke, "We are expected. We are here to see the Witch of Downing Street."

"Yes sir." The guard interrupted. "You may enter." The officer quickly unlocked the gate and allowed us to enter onto Downing Street proper. Not far was another guard standing outside an ornate black door.

"Is this number Ten Downing Street?" I asked my Grandpa.

"Yep. We are almost there, come with me." He smiled and winked at me. I could tell the excitement was building.

Grandpa led us down a narrow passageway between the buildings. It seemed the dark tunnel-like walkway went on as far as the eye could see. Just then, Grandpa stopped and stood tall, "Here. This is the door!"

There, tucked away in this dark and gloomy alley was a distinctive yet unassuming pristine white door. Centered on the door was a rather ghoulish gargoyle head made of brass with a huge circular knocker swinging from its mouth.

Grandpa was smiling from ear to ear as he took the big brass knocker and swung it out and released it so that it banged hard against the door with a thunderous clap.

It seemed as if the door creaked opened as soon as the reverberation from the knocker ceased. There didn't appear to be anyone here to greet us. Grandpa turned to us and whispered, "We have to hurry, and we're almost out of time."

She walked into the room so quietly that I jumped when I noticed her there, dressed from head to toe in white and standing regally before us. I could only look at her in amazement. She wasn't old but she wasn't young. She wasn't beautiful, yet, she wasn't ugly. As a matter of fact, if you were anywhere else, she would have gone completely unnoticed.

No niceties were exchanged. No hellos. No hint at recognition from either Grandpa or the Witch. She held out her hand and opened her fingers. A fine gold chain laced through her fingers and dangling on the end of it was a charm. It was a small replica of an hour glass the size of an old-fashioned matchbox.

"Remember, the twelfth hour on the twelfth day of the twelfth month." I could hear her voice, yet her lips never moved. "You will find the words inscribed on the brass legs that support the glass. Now be on your way, the day is growing older."

Grandpa didn't say a word. He took the chain and amulet from her fingers and placed it around his neck. As soon as he took it from her she seemed to float across the floor and disappeared into the wall.

The door to the gangway opened and before I knew it we were being rushed back out onto the street. No one spoke a word. Grandpa took each of us by the hand and hurried us past the gate guard and back out onto the busy street of Whitehall.

"What was that all about?" Michael was now looking a little flushed.

"She has given me the amulet and the incantation." Grandpa was beginning to show signs of wear. His limp was returning, though he still had enough strength and energy to pull us along with him as we retraced our steps back to the Clock Tower.

Michael and I were huffing and puffing when we finally came to rest against the wall of the tower. Grandpa was fumbling for his glasses.

"What now, Grandpa?" I was growing more confused as time unfolded.

"The Clock Tower holds the biggest time-piece ever created by man." He began to explain. "The city of London was all but lost during the bombings of World War II… all but the mighty clock in this tower! She still tolled the hours, even then, to let the world know there was still hope… this was not the end."

He continued, "The book is magical. I found it years ago in a pile of antiquated books at a dusty old storefront not far from here. I thought it was an old journal that had never been used, and I knew it was special. I paid for it and gave it to your grandmother, she must have put it away to keep and preserve it and I had long forgotten about it until…she died. I was packing her things away when I came across it in one of her old hat boxes."

Grandpa sighed a heavy sigh with the memory and began again, "I am old now. I have lost so much of myself to the years, my hearing, my sight, my mind."

He had a look on his face I had never seen before. He looked frightened.

"My legs don't work anymore, they barely get me where I need to get to..." he smiled and looked over at us for some understanding. "I put my glasses on to look at the book; to see if she had written anything on the pages, I miss her so much."

"You saw the writing then, didn't you Grandpa?" I silently nodded for him to continue.

"Yes. I saw the writing. Such beautiful gold lettering engraved into the soft texture of the leather binding. I opened the book to the first page. It once again announced the books purpose without the mention of who wrote it or to who it was dedicated. The next page held the incantation: Open my eyes, my ears and my mind; show me the treasure I seek to find. The next thing I knew I was standing here beneath the Clock Tower."

"How did you know where to go? What you needed to get back home? You didn't have the book with you anymore and you didn't have your specs." Michael was now showing signs of the same confusion I had been experiencing since we got here.

"There was a man selling nuts on the corner. I could see him clearly. He was standing perfectly still while the others were rushing past him. It was as if he were standing in a time warp that moved at a much slower rate than what everyone else existed in. It appeared that he noticed me in the same way I noticed him. It seemed reasonable to approach him and ask him where I was. But I didn't ask him where I was, what came out was - where am I going. It was all very strange, but the man appeared to know the answer."

"Downing Street. Find the Witch. She has what you need to find the treasure. That's what he said to me as he pointed the way." Grandpa knew he wasn't making any sense to us, but he kept talking.

"There was a woman holding a cat in her arms. Again, she was standing still while the rest of the street was alive with movement. I thought she might be the witch he was talking about. I didn't say a word to her, she simply smiled at me and said, 'approach the gate to Downing Street, tell the guard you are expected as a guest of the Witch.

Look for the black door. Do not enter through that one, you must find the white door. Enter the alleyway, you will see the white door…knock once and it will open. Say nothing. The Witch will meet you and give you an amulet and a spell. Do not tarry. Time is of the essence, as you know. You must get back to the Clock Tower before it strikes the hour.' That was it. She turned and was gone!"

There was a long pause. "Then you caught up to me… how? I don't understand. Now, here we sit waiting for the clock to ring out." Grandpa was beginning to look ill.

"Are you okay, Grandpa?" I asked him.

"I can't hear you as well as I did a moment ago, Marky." He shook his head and was tapping at his ears as if this would restore it. "We have to say the words before it's too late! Marky, here, put my specs on and read the verse, hurry!"

I slipped the glasses on as Grandpa held up the hourglass. There as plain as the nose on my face I could see the writing. But, it wasn't in English or anything I would understand as English. There were symbols etched into the metal:

ΤΑ ΑΥΤΙΑ ΜΟΥ ΑΝΟΙΞΕ...
ΤΗΝ ΨΥΧΗ ΚΑΙ ΤΟ ΜΥΑΛΟ...
ΔΕΙΞΕ ΜΟΥ ΠΟΥ ΘΑ ΒΡΩ ΤΟΝ ΘΗΣΑΥΡΟ

"I can't read it Grandpa!"

I turned the hourglass the other direction and could see letters of the alphabet written in English. I sounded out the words the best I could…

T'aftia mou aneexe...tin pseehee kai to meealo...deexe mou pou tha vro ton theesavro.

Just then, the mighty bell they call Big Ben began to ring out the hours. One...two, the sound was heavy and clear, three...four, Grandpa was screaming into Michaels face, "say it with him!" five...six, "don't lose the glasses, Marky!" All three of us were reciting the verse together, seven...eight... the reverberation of the last peel was hanging in the air around us. It felt like the ground was quaking beneath our feet.

I closed my eyes, I didn't want to see what was about to happen. When the ground settled beneath us and the sound of the bell was no more than a faint echo, I opened them. We were standing next to a gigantic sundial in the middle of ... nowhere.

———◆———

We were together, that was my first concern, second was that we were not at home in our den as I had hoped. We were standing in a field and about 200 yards to our right was what seemed to be the remains of what might have been a place of worship. Michael slowly began looking for clues as to where we were.

The walls of the ruin were collapsing on one side and we could see an altar. On the altar were engravings...I recognized the crescent moon and the sun, but I couldn't make out the other two symbols.

Grandpa must have been reading my mind. "That is the symbol for Alpha and that one is for Omega...the beginning and the end." It was as if he were struck numb by the view.

"Over here!" we heard Michael shout out. "Come look!"

Grandpa and I turned to face the opposite direction, Michael was standing a few yards from us and looking at something shiny lying on the ground; something big.

"What is this?" he asked Grandpa.

"A sundial, it's an ancient time-piece and by the looks of it; Greek." He responded. "The incantation, I think it was Greek also."

Built into the ground on a white marble foundation was the most spectacular thing I had ever seen. It was a huge circular disk with notches all around the circumference of the inner circle and about a foot of ornate symbols decorating the area from the inner circle out to the perimeter of the entire disk. A wedge that resembled a whale's dorsal fin rose up in the center. There were lines radiating from a mark on one side of the disk, and other lines crisscrossing in random order.

"There, see how the shadow from the gnomon, that's the word for this piece here, is cast down this line." Grandpa was pointing to the 'fin' and then tracing the shadow it made down one of the radiating lines. "If we are indeed in Greece, this line indicates that it's eight-o-clock in the morning. The Big Ben had struck its eighth bell when it stopped…makes sense, we were transported here, somewhere in the Greek countryside."

"Grandpa!" Michael grabbed my hand and pulled me to him protectively. "Grandpa, look!"

Standing on the other side of this gargantuan sundial was a dark haired man dressed in white pants and white shirt. The breeze moved through the fabric and made the man look as if he was wearing a silk veil.

"Where are we going?" I heard my Grandpa ask him.

The man pointed to the northeast and replied, "To the ruins of the Palace of Knossos and the Labyrinth of Minos. Do not enter the labyrinth or you will walk the path of the Eternal Perplexities." He then disappeared in the breeze as if he had never been there.

"Grandpa?" Michael asked, "How far is Knossos? Can you walk that far?"

"It is the palace of a king they called Minos. We must be on the island of Crete in Greece. The Cretes, or Minoans as they were once known, are thought to be the oldest civilization on Earth. The Bronze Age began here. Everything about Crete is hidden in legend and oral history. The Minoans were much like the Egyptians in that they used a form of hieroglyphics for written communication. Legend has it that Minos had a labyrinth built there to imprison the Minotaur.

"What is a labyrinth?" I asked.

"What is a Minotaur?" Michael whispered to me.

"It's a life-size maze, Marky, and it's difficult to find your way around in it. We must be careful not to step foot in it just like the man advised.

Then he laughed at Michael who was dumbfounded by all of this. The Minotaur is a man with the head and tail of a bull. Its purpose was to cause terror and the destruction of Crete and Minos had the Minotaur imprisoned in the Labyrinth.

Michael was still standing dumbfounded in spite of Grandpa's lesson.

"Now, let's be on our way," Grandpa urged, "before the sun is high."

We ventured off on our journey to find Knossos. It wasn't far. Just over the hill we saw the palace. Wildflowers bloomed along the rolling hillsides and beyond, as far as the eye could see. We could even see the Aegean Sea from where we stood. The walk down the hillside was easy and the air smelled sweet with the scent of herbs.

As we descended toward the palace we saw the ruins. Could this be what remained of the labyrinth? It was a larger area than I had expected, but then, I don't know what I expected. Grandpa, Michael and I stayed close as we made our way among the stones. Some stone columns were still standing while others lie in pieces upon the ground, weathered and crumbling.

"So, this is the palace?" I asked in a hushed voice.

"Shush, she is here. Don't speak, don't move." Grandpa was scanning the ruins for movement. She appeared just like the man on the hillside did, out of nowhere. She too was wearing white and, oddly, she resembled the Witch of Downing Street, I couldn't be sure, I tried not to look at her directly.

She slowly approached Grandpa and without hesitation, she held out her hand. There, laced between her fingers, was a gold chain with a charm dangling from it.

Again we heard a woman's voice, yet her lips did not move, "Remember, the twelfth hour on the twelfth day of the twelfth month. You will find the words inscribed on the rim of the inner circle, you must be facing True North. Now be on your way, the day is growing older."

Grandpa promptly pulled the chain over his head and placed the odd necklace around his neck where the hourglass was still hanging. He took each of us by the hand once again and led us away, heading back up the hillside from which we came.

"I don't know if I can make it." He was now huffing loudly from the exertion of the climb. "Boys, take me by the arms and pull me along with you. Don't stop until we reach the sundial."

Michael and I weren't much stronger than he was; it took our best efforts to lift him along up the side of the hill. By the time we reached the summit where the dial sat on its massive white throne, we were exhausted and collapsed to the ground.

"What now?" Michael was showing signs of wear and a lack of patience with our Grandpa and his so called 'magic'.

Grandpa caught his breath and began to explain his newly acquired amulet. "This is what they refer to as an equinoctial ring dial. Crete had the advantage of maritime rule and used these to find direction as well as time. It looks a bit like a gyroscope, like the one I bought for you three Christmas' ago. This small slit in the style allows the sun's light to fall on these hour lines here." Our eyes followed his finger nail as he traced the lines on the outer circle.

"What does it say on the inner circle, Grandpa?" My curiosity was now kicking in.

"My specs…do you still have the specs?" He had almost forgotten about them but now it was certain that we needed them if we were going to be able to read the words on the inner ring.

I reached into my pocket and pulled out the glasses once again, and offered them to Grandpa.

"No. You read it Marky, out loud, so we can all say it together." He lifted the amulet up so that I could hold it in my fingers but he did not take the necklace off.

I put the glasses on and looked down at the charm. I couldn't see any writing. "Grandpa, there is nothing written here! I can't see anything!"

"True North!" Michael interjected, "you have to be facing True North!"

Grandpa looked up at the sky for a moment to see which direction the shadow on the sundial had moved to since we had arrived there. "Here, turn this way. Now, see if you can read it."

Sure enough, the words were there. "It's in Greek again, Grandpa…but a little different this time…

Τα αυτιά μου άνοιξε...την ψυχή καιτομυαλό...
Δείξε μου που θα βρώ τον θησαυρό.

I turned a little more to the left and there it was, written in our alphabet!

T'aftia mou aneexe...tin pseehee kai to meealo... deexe mou pou tha vro ton theesavro.

I spoke the words out loud as they appeared. I repeated it again trying to sound out the words correctly. The ground began to vibrate and the air was now swirling around us.

"Say it again! Michael! Say it with us!" Grandpa shouted.

The dust was blowing into my face. And then, as suddenly as it began, it stopped!

———◆———

We were standing in the center of yet another ruin of some kind. "Where are we now, Grandpa?" Michael's eyes were wide in amazement.

"I'm not sure, Michael. Marky? You okay?" Grandpa was concerned now about the toll this was taking on us. "Come on, boys, let's find a place to sit a spell and get our wits about us."

"Don't say that!" I replied with a little bit of an edge to my voice. "Don't say that word – spell."

Grandpa looked over at me and let out a huge sigh. "I never intended for you boys to be involved with all of this. I simply didn't know I was supposed to hold on to my specs…and that useless book." He shrugged and turned away. "Come on, I see a place over here in the shade."

We sat down in the shade of an old abandoned tower. It seemed that everything in Greece was old.

After we caught our breath and relaxed a bit, Grandpa finally spoke up. "If I'm not mistaken, I believe we are sitting in the shadow of the Tower of the Winds. We are still in Greece. In Athens, I'm sure."

"How many more…trips… are we going to take before we can just go… home." I cried. I was beginning to think that this was not going to end well; we may never see Mom or Dad again. The tears fell like rain.

Grandpa put his arm around me, "Please don't cry, Marky. I'll get us back home, I promise. I'll figure this whole thing out and get you both home." He gently and lovingly wiped the tears from my face. "Wait a minute. The clock!"

"Another clock?" I repeated back to him.

"A Water-clock." He corrected. "Michael, come over here, I think I'm starting to see the connection."

"There is a Water Clock inside the tower; a Clepsydra. It measures time with water!" Grandpa was full of renewed vigor. He was pacing back and forth like a young man. "It also displays the seasons of the year and astrological dates, forward and backward! It records the passage of TIME!"

He looked up at the tower again. Jumping and flapping his arms in a fit of excitement he started babbling, "The Tower of the Winds! ...of course!"

"The tower is an octagon," Grandpa continued to explain, " – it has eight sides, one for each of winds – north, northeast, east, southeast, south, southwest, west, northwest… look! At the top of each side is the deity that rules that particular direction. The Wind's source!"

Michael and I jumped up and walked slowly around the marble tower looking up to see the eight gods that were sculpted at the top of each side.

"This is awesome!" Michael exclaimed.

"There use to be a weather vane atop the tower." Grandpa explained, "Triton, and he pointed his mighty rod in the direction that the wind is blowing."

A man walked out from behind a wall we had just viewed. A man in a white robe, of course.

No one said a word. The air around us was like a vacuum and I could barely catch my breath.

Grandpa took a step forward and posed the question once more, "Where are we going?"

"Into the tower." The man replied solemnly. "But do not listen to what your ears hear, nor see what your eyes perceive; be careful what you think, she can read your thoughts. She will ask. Be cautious with your answer. She will be watchful for your true intention." He held out his hand to our Grandpa and there, in his palm, was a compass.

Grandpa opened his hand. The compass lifted out of the man's palm and floated through the air settling gently into the old man's palm.

When I looked back toward the place where the man in white was standing he was no longer there.

Michael knew the next step and ran to one of the iron gates that hung in the doorway of the tower. "It won't open!"

Grandpa ran over to him and pulled him away. "Michael! Listen! We have to be very careful now. Not what your ears hear, your eyes see; be careful what you THINK! She'll know."

We stood there watching our grandfather. He was beginning to age rapidly before our eyes. "Grandpa?" I whispered as I watched him topple to the ground.

"I can't stand anymore, I need help to get into the tower." He coughed out.

Michael and I ran to him and took his arms, lifting him up and moving him toward the tower gate.

"This one didn't open." Michael said, "Let's try another. There are only two entries to the tower, one of them must be the right one and open for us."

"What did you say?" Grandpa turned his head toward Michael. "I can't hear you, speak up."

Michael pulled for us to move toward the next door. "Grandpa, which door?" he yelled.

"We must enter the east door and exit to the west." Grandpa yelled back.

"Is this the east door?" Michael quizzed.

"I can't see the deity from here, I don't know." He opened his hand and gestured to me. "Take the compass, Marky."

Then he reached into his pocket and offered me the glasses. "You'll need these specs if she's in there and offers us another amulet."

I pushed the glasses deep into my pocket. Then I held out the compass. The needle spun round and round and then slowed, finally pointing to Northwest.

"We need to enter into the East doorway – it's this way!" I shouted as I led us to the gate.

I looked once again at the compass to be sure. "It points West, Grandpa" I cried out loudly. Grandpa did not hear. I shouted it out again, "Grandpa, the compass points to the West. Is this the door?"

The double gate began to slowly swing open. I looked at Michael and he nodded in agreement, it was the correct door.

Michael looked at Grandpa with alarm. Then he looked at me and mouthed the words "He cannot see."

I didn't answer. We had to move and we had to move quickly. "Let's go!" I barked. "It's time to go home!"

Together we moved through the doorway and into a room that was approximately 20 feet in diameter and more than double that in height. We could hear the movement of water echoing throughout. Set back near one of the walls were rectangular stones creating a large basin. The walls were decorated with metal symbols and hieroglyphs showing people carrying water vessels. There were water channels and intricate metal devices that moved with the flow of the water. It was an elaborate time-piece; no doubt.

By now Grandpa could not hear us nor could he see. Michael and I were holding him up in a standing position; we were ready to make a quick escape should we need to.

She walked from behind the basin wall. The Witch of Downing Street, the Lady in White at the Sundial, and now another lady dressed in white. She looked much like a nun in habit, her head was covered by a long white shroud; a cloth was wrapped securely around her face and throat. Over this she wore a flowing white robe the length of her stature and then some; it draped onto the floor and pooled around her. All we could see was her face. Her hands were hidden from view beneath the robe's folds.

The sound of water was drowning out my thoughts. I couldn't even hear myself think.

"Michael." I whispered low from the corner of my mouth. God, please let him hear me, I prayed.

"Uh huh..." Without moving his head he turned his eyes in my direction while letting them dart back towards the witch and then back to me.

"Don't listen to what you hear? Don't see with your eyes? Be careful what you think?" I recited to him. "We need to be very careful now or we'll never get home to Mom and Dad."

"Gotcha." He nodded.

The witch was looking through us. It was if she didn't really see us at all.

She spoke without moving her lips. The sound of her voice was coming from every direction. But, I kept my eyes focused on her. "Where are you going?" she asked us.

Michael and I looked at each other. "This isn't supposed to happen, aren't we suppose to ask this question? He whispered over to me.

"Don't say anything, Michael," I hushed back. "Don't think anything."

Grandpa had clearly lost his hearing and his vision was obscured, we saw that happen before we entered the tower, yet before I knew what to say or do, he spoke up.

"Home." He said simply. "We want to go home."

"You must find the Triton." She instructed. She withdrew one hand from the fold in her robe. She was gripping one of the three spindles that supported the frame of an hour-glass; this one was much bigger than the little amulet hanging around Grandpa's neck. It was as tall as the length of my forearm and the globes were the size of small balloons. The metal frame was glistening in the light reflecting from the pool. It was splendid.

"You must have the Triton when you return in one hour if you are to find your way." She advised.

She turned the hourglass over and sat it down on the ground before her. The sand began to seep slowly from the upper bulb, through the small neck connecting it to the empty lower chamber where it began to collect. One hour - *Hour-Glass.*

Again she spoke, "Do not walk into your own shadow. When you stand alone without your 'companion' you will see Triton. Make haste. The hour is upon you. Bring the Triton with you, without it you will be lost forever." "I see you have the book." She let her eyes drop to where I held it in my hands, "how fortunate."

Grandpa made a small motion to move forward and stumbled. Michael and I steadied him and together we slowly inched toward the witch. "Will the book take us home?

"The book will reveal the answer to you when you have the Triton, old man," she nodded towards him and closed her eyes. "The Triton… you will not be able to return without the Triton!"

Michael and I turned Grandpa around and led him back to the west doorway as we had been instructed.

"What is that?" Grandpa muttered. "I can hear something."

"Grandpa? What's wrong?" Michael quickly asked.

"Nothing wrong… I can see…I can see you and I can hear you!" he laughed. "My legs…I think I can walk now."

With that he picked his foot up and placed it down in an effort to take a step. It was like watching a baby learn to walk… then another step and another. Soon Michael and I just looked at each other and shrugged. "We better catch up." Michael said playfully.

We were off on another quest; Triton. How was a weather vane going to help us? I thought as I made it to my Grandpa's side. "Off to find the Wizard, the wonderful Wizard of Oz…" I sang out.

Grandpa had found his cup of youth and we were finding our pace as we headed southward. "Keep the shadow behind you, or something like that…" I told myself.

"The Specs, Marky we need to check the time." He said to me.

I put the glasses on and Grandpa lifted the compass. True North, I turned slightly to make the adjustment, "Aha! True North!"

He took the compass and placed it back into his pocket then lifted the Equinoctial Ring Dial up so I could read it, "It's almost noon, and we must hurry!"

We turned back to the Southwest and picked up the pace. Grandpa was walking like a young lad. There was no hint of the effects of his age about him. He could see, he could hear and he was leading the way!

"Grandpa?" I asked as we were making our way through the terrain. "You couldn't see or hear earlier, and your legs, you seem to get well and then you quickly revert back…it's like you've found the fountain of youth but it only lasts for a while and then…"

"It's the magic, I suppose." He answered back. "It's wonderful. The incantation only gives me a short amount of time. I don't really understand it myself. All I wanted was to be with her again, like it was…" I could hear his voice crack with emotion.

"Our shadows!" Michael shrieked "They're gone!"

"STOP!" Grandpa ordered. "We must stop here and look for it."

"Tell me again, what does it look like?" I asked bemused.

"It's made of bronze, just like the bells of the Bell Tower in London, just like the metal that holds the hourglass amulet, just like the metal of the sundial and the equinoctial ring dial, and the ornamentation on the water clock inside the Tower of the Winds..." Grandpa took the book from Marky and gently stoked the leather cover.

He continued, "He resembles a mermaid in that he is half man and half fish. His left hand is extended over his head and he is pointing to the heavens while the right arm is extended out from his side holding a rod; a spear."

"THERE!" Michael exclaimed.

I looked in the direction that Michael was looking and saw it, leaning against what appeared to be some sort of stone bunker.

Grandpa walked up to where we were standing. "It's a mausoleum." He said in a respectful tone. "The woman they have carved into the stone there, it looks to be Circe of the famous legendary story The Odyssey. She was a powerful witch."

"Wait just a cotton-picking minute!" Grandpa sputtered. "The man in white told us not believe what our eyes see or our ears hear and to be careful what we thought inside the Tower of the Wind; she could read our minds. The witch."

"What does that have to do with this?" I spoke up.

"It was clear that we should be very careful around her. Perhaps she is someone we should be wary of. Perhaps she has another motive for helping me... helping us." he theorized.

"The metal, it's a conductor. Electrical currents can travel through water and through bronze. There are electrical currents in every living thing, including us!" he expounded. "I don't think the Witch is 'alive', nor the man in white. She has given us the amulets and incantations to move between the various places where we would encounter yet another witch, another amulet, and another incantation."

"I don't understand any of this." I said. Michael nodded in agreement. We were indeed lost to his reason.

"Listen." He advised. "We don't have much time. Not far from here is a place known as the Temple of Apollo, it was considered the center of the universe. There is a mark where the eternal flame once burned.

"There were three Pythia or soothsayers, fortune-tellers as we call them." he continued. "The Oracle is a place in Delphi where the Sibyl would go and receive the prophecies."

"Okay, Grandpa," I hurried him along, "We are wasting time... what does this have to do with us?"

"Originally this place was guarded by Python, a child of the Goddess Gaia. However, Apollo destroyed the guardian serpent Python who was swallowed up by a huge fissure in the earth. The body decomposed there, sending toxic fumes into the air above."

He wiped his forehead with the back of his hand. He was perspiring heavily.

"I think we are the pawns in a mythical contest, and they want something from us. I believe they used my weakness, my love for your grandmother, to their own end. They need the weather vane; they need Triton to show them the way." He was beginning to take on the old-man look again as he continued, "They need the bronze amulets to tell them when, where and point the way - but to what?"

"Our shadows, they are returning!" Michael pointed to the ground and then looked back up at Grandpa and me. "Grab the Triton, quick!"

I ran to where the bronze weather vane was propped. Trying not to trip over my own two feet, I snatched up the bronze treasure and ran back to Michael and Grandpa. "Careful! Do not walk into your own shadow!" Grandpa reached out and grabbed my arm pulling me to a halt before I stepped into the silhouette growing bigger on the ground next to me."

"This way," Michael spoke out, "we have to walk this way and head back to the Tower.

Michael looped one of Grandpa's arms and I followed as we moved faster back toward the Tower of the Winds.

That's when it hit me. The book! There must be something in the book that will either take us home or forever trap us in this place, or worse.

"Grandpa, what were you thinking about when you opened the book… in the den, at home?" I was curious to know. After all, Michael and I were trying to find Grandpa when we opened it, and it took us to where we could find him… our treasure.

He hesitated for a moment but returned to his hurried pace. "I wanted to go back to the time I met your grandmother, I wanted to see her again, relive the wonderful life we had together." He was now crying noticeably. I could hear the sobs along with his breathlessness.

"That's it! Grandpa, you met Grandma in England. She helped out in the American Red Cross there, remember? You met when you were on the last leg of your journey back home from the war in Korea. She got on the plane with you! Remember?" I was all but spitting the words out as I tried to remember the story told to me all these years.

"Yes!" Grandpa stopped cold. That's right! I wanted to return to England; to my beautiful Annie." he was trying to stop the tears from falling. "They were rioting in the streets chanting 'Peace'. The police were three deep and clubbing them to keep them off Downing Street. I saw Anne standing in the crowd of protesters crying. I made my way to her and saw that her knees were bleeding and she was frightened so I scooped her up and pushed our way back out of the angry mob."

He took a deep breath and continued walking and telling his story, "I took her for a cup of tea to calm her at a small Inn five or so blocks away. We talked all night…" he was faltering as he continued to fight his emotions, though they were already winning, "I talked her into marrying me that night! I bought our tickets to come home with the little money I had left…"

"What time is it?" Michael asked hysterically. "We have to run!"

"No. Wait a sec." Grandpa collected himself and asked Marky for his specs. He smiled as his fingers traced the lettering that could only be seen through those lenses, "The Treasure of Time."

He opened the book to the second page where the verse would be found. "There is…the incantation. Open my eyes…"

"Stop Grandpa!" I screamed as I took the book from his hands. "Don't read it. What are you thinking about right now? We have to be careful, remember?"

We heard a woman's laughter echoing through the air. We all spun around to look for the source. "We have to get back to the Tower." Grandpa said firmly. We have to have all the pieces together, I'm sure of it."

———◆———

We moved as fast as we could to get to the tower door. "Enter from the East!" Michael yelled as we made our way to the correct door.

We all pushed past the iron gates and came to an abrupt halt in front of the Water-clock. Standing in the shallow pool that was being fed into the complex mechanisms set to keep the time, was the Witch.

"I gave you all what you asked for. It's too late to change things now, give me the amulets and the book, they won't help you now." This time she was actually spitting the words from her mouth.

"Don't do it, Grandpa." I pleaded. "The book and the charms must still be powerful or she wouldn't want them so badly. If she is a real witch she wouldn't have to ask for them" I reasoned.

Sparks emanated from the waters and bounced off the metal objects surrounding the pool. "Give it to me. They are of no use to you." She commanded him again.

Grandpa turned his head towards Michael and me and mouthed the words "I can't see. I can't hear." With that, we watched as he fell to the ground.

"Grandpa!" Michael called out as he reached out trying to catch him.

I saw his glasses fall out of his pocket and crash to the floor next to him. Oh, no! I thought to myself as I quickly dived to the floor for them. "I have them! I have the glasses Grandpa." I yelled to the man crumpled on the floor.

"The book!" Michael reminded me. "Get the book!"

As I was about to grab the book the pages automatically opened up for me. I fumbled with the glasses and managed to get them on. There on the page was a verse, but it didn't look like any language I'd ever seen:

DNIF OT KEES I ERUSAERT EHT EM WOHS.
DNIM YM DNA SRAE YM, SEYE YM NEPO.

"I can't read it, Michael" I said defeated. "I don't know what it says."

"Do not listen to what your ears hear, nor see what your eyes perceive…" out of nowhere came the haunting voice of the man in white.

"I can't see him, Michael. Do you see him?" I called out. "Where is he?" I pulled the book to my chest and crawled over to where my brother and grandfather huddled close.

"Be careful what you think, she can read your thoughts. She will ask. Be cautious with your answer." The voice resonated.

The witch laughed and threw her head back. "Apollo, you are such a spoiler."

She turned to face us again. "Where are you going?" she posed.

No one spoke.

"Where are you going?" she demanded again.

I can't answer it, I thought to myself. I don't know how to answer.

Michael was holding Grandpa's head to his shoulder and looking all the more worried as I struggled with the question. I kept rolling the possible answers in my mind, I could say home but then, what would that mean to her? Where would it really take us? Where is home? I just don't know how to answer the question.

Again she queried, "Where are you going? Speak it!" she roared.

The floor of the Tower was beginning to vibrate beneath us. "I haven't given you my answer!" I screamed into the room.

"The Triton!" Michael sputtered. "Where is it? It's not here!" He was visibly shaking now and holding Grandpa tightly.

I searched the room from where I knelt looking to the East door of the Tower of the Winds. "There!" I screeched loudly, "just inside the East gate."

I placed the glasses securely into my pants pocket and put the leather-bound book into my shirt. I could feel its warmth on my skin. Slowly and carefully I began to crawl across the floor toward the Triton.

Hissssss. This was a new but familiar sound. Hissssss. The sound was clearer.

"Marky! Look!" I heard Michael squeal in a high-pitched frantic scream.

"She is changing!" He screamed again. He began to rock himself and Grandpa on the floor. He had a look of terror on his face that contrasted the disturbingly serene look on Grandpa's face.

I looked over to the Water-clock and couldn't believe my eyes. In the space where the witch had been standing was now a gigantic snake! She had transformed herself there...I was frozen in fear.

The room began to fill with dust as the wind began swirling into and around the interior of the tower. I could feel the dampness in the air as the winds picked up the water in its fury.

The Triton! I crawled faster to the gate with the East wind blowing hard against my face. I felt the cold metal in my hand. I had it! With the Triton in hand I turned to crawl back to Michael and Grandpa.

She was coiled and her head was looming over me as if she were about to strike. Instinctively I braced myself and held the Triton out in front of me to block her. I turned my head and closed my eyes as I heard the awful bellowing cry coming from the monster. She had indeed recoiled to strike with all her might, but had met with the spear of the Triton before reaching me.

I watched in horror as she threw her head from side to side trying to dislodge the Triton from her throat. The floor was swaying to and fro more violently than before. The ground ripped opened beneath her and swallowed her into its deep chasm before finally coming to a rest once again. The wind came to rest also and I could see Grandpa and Michael lying on the ground in front of me.

"Michael! Gran…," I was cut short by the voice of the man - the man in white – Apollo.

"You have destroyed her." He said.

"I didn't mean to, she was going to kill me, I was just trying to block her." I sobbed in defense.

"I destroyed her sister, Pythia, at Delphi, but Myra had gotten away from me." His voice was not coming from out there, in the room, but inside of my head. I could hear him speaking inside of me.

I didn't speak but thought my question, *Who are you*.

He answered, *I am Apollo, God of Prophecy, God of Reason and of Light*.

I could not believe my ears. But of course! I'm not supposed to believe what my ears were hearing. I was now listening with my mind. I was conversing with a god… in my mind!

Was it you who sold nuts on the corner in London? I inquired telepathically.

It was I. he responded and added, *That whom you met and is known as the 'Witch of Downing Street' is better known as the 'Hours'. She provided the measure of time. She interceded on your Grandfather's behalf. Myra was in search of the Navigator. She needed the* NAVIGATOR.

Needed him for what? I volleyed back to him.

The Navigator is needed to find the **Way**. He riddled in return.

Who was the woman at Crete? I asked in my thoughts.

"She is called 'Destiny'." He answered aloud. "She reveals the true path, the Navigator must make the choice."

Path… like, where to go? which direction? I pondered to myself forgetting for a moment that he could hear my thoughts.

"The Navigator; he possesses the compass and will choose the path." He replied to my surprise.

"And the woman, here, why did she need the charms if she had the magic? What was she going to do with them?" I asked to him.

"She was searching for the amulets in order to resurrect her sister from the bowels of the earth. She would need the items and the Navigator to direct her to through the depths of the Underworld and into Hades and then to bring them both back safely." He explained.

"But the 'Navigator'; er…Grandpa…," I stammered, "he is old and can't see very well with his specs on, and much less without them…"

"No, young man, it isn't your Grandfather she needed." He interrupted.

"Then… who?" I asked. "Who is the Navigator then?"

"You are the Navigator" he answered. "You are the chooser. Your Grandfather understood this, though he was not aware. It was you, and only you, who could interpret the inscriptions."

"Me?" I said in shocked disbelief. "I don't know how to navigate or choose or whatever it is you say I'm supposed to do."

I could hear his laughter ringing clear inside my head. *Take the compass, young man, and navigate!*

"No!' I said out loud again. "I told you, I don't know how." I continued to crawl to my Grandpa and brother as they lie motionless on the dusty floor. Carefully I reached out to feel if Michael was breathing and then to check if Grandpa was alive. I began to cry. "I can't do this. I can't navigate. I'm just a boy."

"I was just a boy when I slay the dragon Python." He reassured me. "I'll start you on your way, but only you can choose."

Apollo began his instruction, "The compass will show you the direction, coming or going, and you must begin your journey the moment you turn the hourglass over. You only have one minute of one hour to gather your bearings and choose."

He paused so I could put the instructions to memory and continued, "You must choose the path. You may go forward into time or backward. You have one minute of one hour to decide and choose."

Again he gave pause so that I could process the information, then he began to speak again, "The Equinoctial Ring will show you the longitude and the latitude, as well as the time at the destination of your choosing. Hold the ring to True North and it will guide you there."

"I don't think I can remember all of this." I shook my head as if to put it all in right order.

"Listen to me, Navigator," this was the first time he had referred to me by this formal sounding title. "The glasses will help you to see and the book is your vessel."

145

"I don't understand." I was trying to absorb it all. I knew I was the only one who could save Michael and Grandpa now. I had to get it right. I had to choose wisely.

"Okay." I said to him. "I can do this. What comes next?"

He came out from behind the stone Water-clock and approached me. I was not afraid. The man in white, Apollo, stood before me in the Tower of the Wind. He spoke out loud so that I could hear with my ears as well as my mind. "The Gods of the Eight Winds will rush upon you. They will confuse you. You must take the Triton with you."

He held out the weather-vane that had been plunged into the neck of the dragon-snake. "I plucked it from her as she fell into the abyss." He answered my un-asked question. "Take it with you. Once you have spoken the word you will need to point Triton's staff in the direction you wish to go. It will pierce the wind and show you the 'Way'. Close your eyes - close your ears – listen to the *words* and see the *way*."

I took the Triton and held it close. He reached out with both arms and placed his hands upon my shoulders. "The weight of their life and yours rests on these, Godspeed." He winked at me and disappeared before my eyes.

"No…" I whispered softly.

I looked over at Grandfather and Michael lying on the floor. They looked as if they were in a peaceful sleep. They were unaware of the events that had transpired since the serpent had appeared. A shiver ran up my spine and I shook it off. I knew that our fate was now in my hands; the hands of a ten year old boy.

"I can do this!" I said to myself. "I just have to remember…"

I carefully removed the two pendants from around Grandpa's neck. There was absolutely no reaction to indicate he was waking. I placed the chains around my own neck. The weight of the amulets was heavier than I imagined.

The compass! I reminded myself. I found Grandpa's pocket and reached in; nothing. So I turned him a bit and squeezed my hand into the other pocket... I was elated when my fingers connected with the cold metal of the compass. I withdrew it and stared down at this magnificent jewel.

"Compass – check, Hour-glass – check, Ring – check, Glasses..." I dug into my own pocket and pulled out Grandpa's bent specs. I placed them securely onto my face and pulled the book from its hiding place inside my shirt. The rush of the cool air against the warmth of where the book hugged my chest felt nice. "Glasses, Book – check, check!"

I laid the book on the cold marble floor of the Tower of the Winds and watched in amazement as the pages blew open and came to rest on a page with ENGLISH written upon it. I stood up tall and proud looking down at the open pages of the book.

"OPEN MY EYES, MY EARS AND MY MIND – SHOW ME THE TREASURE I SEEK TO FIND" I said in my most 'Navigator-like voice'.

I heard something move behind me. It was Grandpa! He and Michael were waking up. "Grandpa" I rejoiced... "Michael!"

The air in the room began to spin, picking up the dust and swirling it about. "Quick! Michael! Help Grandpa up and stand here with me. Don't ask questions, just do it!"

Michael wasn't about to argue, the scene he was waking up to must have seemed like the continuation of the dream he passed out from. Michael lifted Grandpa and placed his arm around him for support. "We are going HOME!" I said with confidence.

I have only one minute each to mark the time, decide on the direction, get the coordinates of our destination, speak the incantation...and what...?

I held the compass out so I could see it and issued my first 'order'. Compass! Show me the direction – we are GOING home! The needle spun around under the glass and came to rest on 'W'. The dust and wind began blowing from the East door and exiting out the West door of the Tower. I quickly put the compass into my pocket and reached down to find the equinoctial ring dangling from its chain. I pulled it over my head and held it out so that I could see the markings on the bronze metal rings.

"Show me the longitude and latitude and the time. Our destination: Sparta Wisconsin, USA – 12:00 p.m. December 12," I commanded. The rings of the amulet began to spin and came to rest on 43°56'00N Latitude 090°49'00W longitude, 11:55 a.m. CST/ UTC. "Mark it" I ordered again placing the ring into my other pocket.

Fifty-five minutes, I thought about it for a second…That's right! …5 minutes…I have to hurry, "Mark it."

I lifted the Hourglass from around my neck and kissed it for luck before turning it over and laying it next to the book. "Okay now, Grandpa, Michael – repeat the spell after me: Open my eyes, my ears and my mind – show me the treasure I seek to find."

Together we spoke the incantation again – "Open my eyes, my ears and my mind – show me the treasure I seek to find."

The Tower was now spinning opposite the direction of the wind and it was making me incredibly dizzy. "Hold on everybody, here we go!" I called out to Michael and Grandpa. The winds picked us up and carried us through the West gate of the tower. We were on our way…Sparta, Wisconsin – December 12 – just in time for lunch!"

"Wha…What year, Marky. What YEAR?" Grandpa's voice was crackling as he forced the words out.

"Year?" I forgot the year!!! I dug both hands into both pockets and felt for the ring. My left hand found it. I pulled it out and held it out to see… 1951, that can't be – we weren't even born yet!"

Michael yelled out against the wind, "Give it the right year Marky, quick!"

"Show me the longitude and latitude and the time. Our destination: Sparta Wisconsin, USA – 12:00 p.m. December 12 - **2012**," I commanded. The rings of the amulet began to spin and came to rest again on the same coordinates and time of day and now I could read the correct year – 2012. "Mark it. Mark it. Mark it." I screamed.

The air shifted so violently that it almost knocked us off of our feet. I immediately put my arm around the other side of Grandpa and helped Michael bolstered him up and to keep him steady.

I closed my eyes and prayed. "Please God, take us home."

Grandpa moaned and whispered over to me, "Where am I going?"

"Home" I replied.

"And, Annie?" he asked opening his eyes to watch my expression, a tear tracing down his face.

"I don't know where Grandma is anymore. She died Grandpa, remember?" I delicately answered him.

He closed his eyes and another tear fell, and another…

I lifted the chain over my head and placed it with the amulet around his neck. Then I reached into my pocket and pulled out the compass… "Here Grandpa, you're going to need this too." I placed it in his hand and he squeezed his fingers around it.

I took the specs from my face and placed them securely onto his. "You might need these to read the charms and maybe, even… SEE her – Give Grandma a kiss for us…" I watched as the corners of his mouth turned up into a smile and he opened his eyes once again.

"I love you boys - with all my heart." He choked out. "My days are at an end. I just want to be with my Annie. Do you understand?"

Michael and I both answered at once, "Yes, Grandpa, we understand." Michael hugged Grandpa tight and I could see he was crying. I wiped the tear from my eye and hugged him around the other side.

All of the sudden we felt Grandpa stand on his own. He looked at us through the specs and then took them off, folded them and placed them in his shirt pocket. "I might need these later, but right now I can see you and hear you just fine... thank you, boys. You've made all my dreams come true. Tell your Mom and Dad someday about our last adventure together and tell your Mother – she made us proud, gave us the two BEST treasures any Grandparent could ask for – and, please, tell her I love her."

The three of us hugged tightly one last time. Grandpa stepped over the book and turned to face me.

"You must tell the winds where to carry me, son. They are at your command and will listen only to your voice. Remember – London England, the 12th hour of the 12th day of the 12th month – 1950!

I instructed the winds to take our Grandfather to his destination in time and where to drop him off.

We watched as a vortex of wind separated us there and pulled him off into another direction. Both Michael and I were sobbing into each other shoulders. He was gone.

Lifting the Triton up and into the wind, we headed for home.

———◆———

"Boys, he has gone on to a better place. He's with Grandma now. That's where he has always been the happiest, with his Annie. Let's be happy for him." It was Dad's voice!

I looked up and we were standing in the chapel in front of our Grandpa's casket. He looked so...peaceful, like he was having the sweetest of dreams. I could smell the wild-flowers mixed with herbs.

I looked at Michael and both of us beamed our biggest smiles and hugged while we jumped for joy! Dad looked at us like we had lost our minds. "What…the…"

"We're home!" Michael exclaimed. "That's all that matters now, we are all together and…

I finished his sentence, "Grandpa is home in his heaven, with Grandma by his side."

Mom smiled at us and came over to give us each a big hug. "Of course, we are blessed to have our family together and safe." She said. Then she turned around and leaned down to kiss Grandpa's face, "Wherever you are Dad, I hope you are safe with Mom. May God bless us all, in this life and in the next."

She opened her arms and waved us to join her and Dad as we walked to the back of the chapel and out the…West entrance…toward the future.

Somewhere in London England, December 12, 1950 – Frank and Anne are sipping their tea and falling in love.

VEIL OF AUTUMN

There is a chill in the room today. Autumn makes a grand entrance as she dances upon the mist and beats her tambourine. Round and round she spins in twirls, swirls, dips, and lifts; the rustle of her colorful skirt illuminated by the morning sun.

I watch from the window. The pane rattles with anticipation as she rustles by, playing peek-a-boo with the lace curtains hanging there. I hear the hushed whispers, telling secrets and then, the howling laughter. A shiver runs the length of my spine. Where is my shawl…?

Who? She asks as she taps at my door. Whooooo?

I don't remember. Something stops me cold as I step toward the threshold; wanting to open it for her but dread fills my veins and I am frozen in fear.

I don't know who. I only know the room is becoming colder, musty and damp. Again I feel the icy fingers running up and down my back; I shiver.

From behind the veil I watch the hours play games in the shadows running through the tall grass that was once a handsome lawn where we played croquet.

The Red Maples that line the meandering drive to our front door are set ablaze in the twilight. Flaming embers soon cover the ground.

As dusk approaches, the playful breezes turn sinister and foreboding. Their sharp tongues cut through the tree limbs like a knife. Detached, I stand watching with morbid captivation. The branches moan under the assault. Blood sprays into the air, falling like a tortured rain to form pools of crimson scarlet on the ground below.

Who? The wind wails as it beats upon my door. Whooo?

Who indeed!

Faces appear upon the window glass, painted in frost and howling from the pain of the changing.

I cannot let you in. Detached!…I am stolid, unaffected, numb…

I cannot escape these unhallowed hollow walls. I wear them like a shroud to shelter me from the mocking winter as he approaches. No, I will not open the door for the season though she amuses and confuses the senses. I will not welcome her in so she can distract me whilst the frigid grip of death tightens around my neck. I will not surrender to mortality!

The night covers the landscape like a pall. Darkness and the creatures that haunt within are my only companions. I, in my mantilla, shall ascend the grand staircase and retire to my chamber and awaken to my mourning; forever in autumn.

ABOUT THE AUTHOR

M. Teresa Clayton is the author of *Mystic Verses*, *…And The Snow Falls*, as well as a children's book *The Garden of Secret Wishes*.

She calls Missouri home and greets each new day with her husband Jim, their two dogs and four cats.

Her children and grandchildren keep her grounded, the 'adopted' children she calls her Lovelies surround her with light, and the storytellers she lovingly refers to as the *Others* take her beyond the veil where she plays in mystical realms.

INTRODUCING R. L. HODGE

Horror- Fantasy artist RL Hodge was born on March 10th, 1966 in Cincinnati, Ohio. Today, he makes his home and studio in Sevierville, Tennessee with his wife Ann and their one eared cat, Mr. Kitty. He is also the proud father of one son, Logan, from a previous marriage.

Though Mr. Hodge studied fine art for two years at the Art Institute of Cincinnati, he also considers himself largely a self-taught artist. He now crafts his original works of art with a mixed media technique involving digital and traditional styles. Earlier works were done with pencils, watercolor and ink.

He began his art career in 1993 doing comic book and T-Shirt art. Much to his surprise, the interest in his Horror - Fantasy art seemed to increase very quickly once he showcased his art in a local comic shop. He expanded to include conventions and the web after several well know artists (Tim Bradstreet, David Mack, and Jeff Smith) viewed his work and convinced him to take a more serious outlook on the world of art and "To make your mark..." - David Mack of Kabuki fame.

He is perhaps most known for his ability to capture the haunting and often mysterious beauty of scenes totally opposite of reality. Each of his visions brought to life on the digital canvas have a personality of their own, evoking strong feelings in those who view them. Some of his characters are elegant, soft and full of splendor, while others are defiant, dark and deadly.

When asked about the path he chose to follow with his art, RL Hodge had this to say..."I didn't choose to paint images of dark fantasy for my art career. It honestly never seemed like a choice, more like I was destined. From the time I was a young boy, I fell in love with the Universal Monster Movies, Creepy and Eerie magazines, and fantasy art, especially art centered on the things that go bump in the dark. I am inspired by many things...books, movies, music, and my nightmares. I hope that my artwork serves to remind others of the darkness that surrounds us and lives within us always." - RL Hodge

"The art of RL Hodge captures the stark reality of your dreams and then twists them into something eerie and frightening. Then he turns and snatches a nightmare or two and casts a romantic dreamlike spell that makes it all seem right." – M Teresa Clayton, author of MYSTIC VERSES.

Learn more about this artist by visiting   www.rlhodge.com

159